camp
CONFIDENTIAL

D0109405

Alex's Challenge

GROSSET & DUNLAP
Published by the Penguin Group
Penguin Group (USA) Inc., 375 Hudson Street, New York, New York 10014, U.S.A.
Penguin Group (Canada), 10 Alcorn Avenue, Toronto, Ontario, Canada M4V 3B2
(a division of Pearson Penguin Canada Inc.)
Penguin Books Ltd, 80 Strand, London WC2R ORL, England
Penguin Ireland, 25 St Stephen's Green, Dublin 2, Ireland
(a division of Penguin Books Ltd)
Penguin Group (Australia), 250 Camberwell Road, Camberwell, Victoria 3124, Australia
(a division of Pearson Australia Group Pty Ltd)
Penguin Books India Pvt Ltd, 11 Community Centre, Panchsheel Park,
New Delhi – 110 017, India
Penguin Group (NZ), Cnr Airborne and Rosedale Roads, Albany, Auckland 1310, New
Zealand (a division of Pearson New Zealand Ltd)
Penguin Books (South Africa) (Pty) Ltd, 24 Sturdee Avenue, Rosebank,
Johannesburg 2196, South Africa

Penguin Books Ltd, Registered Offices:
80 Strand, London WC2R ORL, England

If you purchased this book without a cover, you should be aware that this book is stolen property. It was reported as "unsold and destroyed" to the publisher, and neither the author nor the publisher has received any payment for this "stripped book."

The scanning, uploading, and distribution of this book via the Internet or via any other means without the permission of the publisher is illegal and punishable by law. Please purchase only authorized electronic editions, and do not participate in or encourage electronic piracy of copyrighted materials. Your support of the author's rights is appreciated.

Copyright © 2005 by Grosset & Dunlap. All rights reserved. Published by Grosset & Dunlap, a division of Penguin Young Readers Group, 345 Hudson Street, New York, New York 10014. GROSSET & DUNLAP is a trademark of Penguin Group (USA) Inc. Printed in the U.S.A.

Library of Congress Cataloging-in-Publication Data

Morgan, Melissa J.
  Alex's challenge / by Melissa J. Morgan.
    p. cm. — (Camp confidential ; 4)
  Summary: During the last weeks of summer camp, eleven-year-old Alex Kim has trouble hiding a secret from the other girls in bunk 3C while also trying to meet the high standards she sets for herself in sports, relationships, and other activities.
  ISBN 0-448-43876-3 (pbk.)
  [1. Camps—Fiction. 2. Friendship—Fiction. 3. Secrets—Fiction. 4. Diabetes—Fiction. 5. Perfectionism (Personality trait)—Fiction.] I. Title. II. Series.
  PZ7.M82545Al 2005
  [Fic]—dc22
                        2005005344

10 9 8

camp CONFIDENTIAL

Alex's Challenge

by Melissa J. Morgan

Grosset & Dunlap

Dear Bridgette,

I'm still here at Camp Lakeview. Just two more weeks left before we can hang out—in person—again! I'm so excited to see you.

Thanks for the letters and manga books you've been sending me. I'm really trying to love anime as much as you do, and I'm getting into some of it. When I read that last one, I thought of you the whole time. I love how the Ninja Supertwins trick their kidnapper into letting them go. You're just like the brainy one (I'm the one who can fly and do flips and stuff—ha ha ha). It's fun to imagine that you're right here with me.

But you're not.

Do you know how much I miss you?

Brynn and I have been keeping busy—we're always swimming or jumping rope or staying up way too late. She can be a handful, though, always wanting me to practice lines with her (you know, she's a literal drama queen) and to help her find the stuff she lost in our big old bunk. I'd like to see her practice soccer with me! She doesn't like sports all that much, and, as you know, I live for anything athletic.

We're so different that sometimes I can't believe we're such good friends.

How's summer practice been without me? If I come back and you're a whole lot better than I am, you're just going to have to teach me your new moves. Deal?

I'm learning some new stuff—from boys, of all people. I get to play with the counselors a lot, which makes me better. But sometimes, I think they let me score points when they shouldn't. I'm not complaining, though. I'm having a blast. Anyway, I can't wait to play with you!

Just know that I miss you and think of you all the time. You don't know how much I wish you were here right now! Ugh. I don't have to pretend around you. You know how it is.

I miss you. Did I say that already? Well, I just said it again!

Best Friends Forever,
Alex

Alex had just gotten into bed and was trying to relax. If only her brain had an off switch! She was deep in thought, wishing she could be one of the Ninja Supertwins. She wished she could just have special powers so her life would be easier. Every time she hit the soccer field, she had to score at least three points for her team. Every time she left the bunk, she had to worry if she'd stay strong for the rest of the day. And every time her camp friends had issues—like when Jenna thought Chelsea had tripped her at lunch—they looked to Alex to keep the peace. Alex couldn't understand why she felt so much pressure and where it was all coming from.

At that moment, Jenna was causing Alex's stress. Jenna was addicted to sugar, and her parents liked to feed that addiction with packages from home. Sometimes, Jenna got cupcakes. Other times, she passed out Swedish fish. That night, she had the largest quantity of Nerds that Alex had ever seen. The round, little balls of candy were pink and purple. As Jenna passed them around—she was totally generous—some Nerds inevitably went flying. Gnat-sized streaks of unnatural color dashed through the air like Fourth of July sparklers.

Alex couldn't help herself; she peeked up from her

letter to watch the scene, her mouth beginning to water. She loved the sharp-sweet flavor of Nerds. Just as she was going back to writing, a handful of the hard sugar pellets nicked her left cheek.

"Agh!" Alex yelled. Those buggers were dangerous.

Some girls started to grumble while others laughed. After six weeks together, everyone knew who'd get cranky (Chelsea) versus who'd get goofy (Jenna, Grace, Natalie). That's what had happened at Camp Lakeview every year Alex had been there, and she'd been going there for a lonnnggg time. The girls grew "thisclose," and sometimes there was this magical warm and fuzzy feeling between them, like you'd met eleven soul mates. Other times, during the War of the Nerds, for example, "thisclose" was a recipe for calorie-infused disaster.

"Hey, did you get any?" Valerie whispered to Alex.

"Yeah, they left bruises on my cheek," Alex said, passing up the sweet treats as usual. This time, Alex went back to writing for real. She started on another letter to her soccer coach. She had to concentrate on seeming busy so the girls would be less likely to pay attention to her. Alex wouldn't disturb a fly—and she liked herself that way. She was the original get-along girl who never instigated feuds or showed up late. She didn't even yell at Jenna's twin brother, Adam, when he pranked the bunk—leaving fake bugs on all the girls' pillows. Though that prank was pretty irritating, not to mention uninspired. Except for Brynn, who was her best camp friend, most people didn't know what made Alex tick. And sometimes even Brynn didn't know.

"Okay, cool," Val said. "More for me then."

"I *know* you didn't just hit me in the eye!" Chelsea yelled into the air. Lights-out was in fifteen minutes, but she was always in bed first. She claimed that her face broke out if she didn't get enough beauty sleep. Chelsea even tried to get the other girls to quiet down early, as if that ever worked.

"Aye aye, Captain Chelsea," Grace mimicked. "You'd better watch out, or you might lose a tongue, too."

"Grace, please stop," Chelsea said.

"Oh, we're just having fun," Jenna added. With so many brothers and a sister, she was pretty good at keeping the peace—as long as she wasn't doing battle with Adam.

"Well, not to be a party pooper," said Natalie, "but I stayed up way too late doing everyone's nails last night." Alex didn't let Natalie put all that colored gunk on her hands or face; makeup just seemed hot and slimy. But Alex did love Natalie nevertheless, who was the daughter of the mega-star Tad Maxwell. *Tad Maxwell!* Alex had taken down her posters of him after she'd found out Natalie's news at the beginning of the summer. It was way too weird to worship her friend's dad. Though Natalie's father *was* the most amazing athlete Alex had ever seen on screen— he even did most of his own stunts in the *Spy* movies. Alex's favorite scene was when Tad jumped off Mount Fuji when the deranged monk was chasing him. Anyway, Alex had to hand it to Natalie; Natalie wasn't stuck-up or glamorous or Hollywood at all. Even if Natalie did love teen magazines, she was down-to-earth.

"Boo!" said Alyssa, Natalie's best friend at camp. Alyssa, a funky, artsy girl, hurled a few more candies at Chelsea teasingly.

"I *said* stop it," Chelsea yelled again. Brynn and Grace talked about the summer play again, and that made the others girls roll their eyes. Natalie put her head under her pillow to avoid all the noise. Jessie and Candace started whining about how hot it was, and Valerie and Sarah started singing "My Dog Has Fleas" for absolutely no good reason. Despite the colorful Nerds that had just been launched around the room, the girls seemed only blue.

Alex just didn't get it. She wondered why it was that every year, people got down in the dumps toward the end of camp. It was that weird time where kids weren't glowing from the newness of Lakeview anymore, and Color War was still a little bit too far away to get excited about. Plus, the kids all knew one another well enough to get touchy about the slightest things. Natalie was worried about Simon, who hadn't looked for her during free period that day. Grace complained about her parents, who were making her read *The Jungle Book*. Chelsea whined that her skin was oily (it so wasn't—no matter how mean she was, she was still super pretty). Brynn didn't know how on Earth she'd memorize all of her lines in time to perfect the voice she needed to deliver them. Alex, of course, had offered to help out as usual.

Alex breathed in deeply, trying not to get teary. She knew it wasn't nice of her to be jealous of them, but she was. She would've traded any one of their problems—she would even take two or three of their issues at once!—to get rid of her own. She wanted to know what it was like to be concerned about stuff you could actually do something about. She would've given her athletic ability—all of it— for just one day where she didn't have to worry, worry, and worry some more. There she was with the girls who knew her best, if anyone knew her at all, and still, Alex felt totally alone.

Chelsea, surprisingly, had risen from bed and walked over to Jenna's bottom bunk in her pink-feathered night slippers that her mom had just sent her. She went back to her bed proudly because she had just scored a new handful of Nerds.

"You want some?" she asked Alyssa, thrusting her hand toward Alyssa's face. Alyssa turned the other way, which was the smart thing to do. If Alyssa had said yes, Chelsea would've yanked her hand away. The girls could handle Chelsea because at least her behavior was predictable.

"You want some?" Chelsea asked, shoving the Nerds in Alex's face next.

Alex didn't appreciate the interruption. She was busy thinking and pretending to write her letter. She tried to ignore Chelsea, but it didn't work.

"I *said*," Chelsea repeated, "would you like some?"

Alex tried to be as casual and distracted as she could when she gave her usual answer, "No, thank you." She started scribbling words onto her sheet of paper energetically. She wanted to look inspired so no one would dare break her train of thought. No one would have, either—no one except Chelsea.

"What? Are you watching your weight?" Chelsea said, heading back to her own bed again and dragging her pink slippers. Under her breath, she added, "Maybe you're like one of those girls in the sappy teen magazine articles with an eating disorder."

The rest of the bunk gasped, especially Brynn. Alex knew it was because Chelsea had been brazen enough to verbalize what everyone else had been thinking all summer long. Everyone wondered why she didn't partake during bunk parties, but Chelsea was the only one rude enough to actually bring it up.

"Maybe you should mind your business," Brynn said to Chelsea in defense of her friend. Alex thought Brynn would sneak over to talk about it, but much to Alex's relief, she didn't. Instead, Brynn whispered something to Sarah. At that moment, Alex felt so weird, so out of touch with everyone.

"Well, okay then," Chelsea said. "Hey, everyone, maybe we should try to be as slim and trim and perfect as Alex," she added as Brynn shot her a dirty look. Alex clasped her pen so tightly that she thought it might snap in half. She poked a hole through her letter by accident. She wanted to scream, to rip Chelsea's slippers to shreds. But mostly, she just hoped that no one could tell how fed up she was getting of everyone wondering what was wrong.

"Just ignore her," Valerie interrupted.

So that's what Alex did, for the moment at least. Staying quiet was easier this time. Infuriated and nervous, she thought about how she had been born with a petite Korean body like her mother's. She thought about eating and how much it terrified her. Since food was definitely an issue for her these days, she had diverted more energy than ever to working out. Alex felt more powerful when she had strong muscles, quick running reflexes, and expert soccer abilities. She was willing to do anything to have those skills. She focused on those thoughts, trying not to think about what Chelsea had just said.

But Alex could barely stand it. She was ready to shout at Chelsea, to tell her what a witch she was for always getting into other people's business and making a big deal about herself. And Chelsea wasn't the only one who would feel Alex's wrath. Alex was ready to tell her whole bunk to just cheer up. She held herself back and got her thoughts organized. Alex never spoke without getting it together first. Her mom and dad had taught her to be smooth and cool and collected, and most of the time, that's exactly what Alex was. But then, with the Nerds fresh on her mind and Chelsea right there in her face, Alex just about exploded—until Julie, their counselor, and Marissa, their counselor in training (CIT)—arrived in the bunk after their staff meeting.

"Lights out!" Julie yelled. Surely, she'd heard the commotion and that's why she had butted in—it seemed like Julie was always coming to the rescue.

Alex was thankful. In her heart, she had wanted to lose it on everyone. But her mind knew better. Starting something with the whole rest of her bunk—girls she loved, well, most of the time—was a disaster waiting to happen. Alex looked up and noticed that all eyes were on her. She hoped they hadn't been able to tell that she was about to lose her temper. Alex's skin turned redder and redder—now because she was angry and embarrassed. Before anyone could say another word, Valerie got out of bed and flicked the lights off fast—it was like she'd been reading Alex's mind. The tension in the room went from thick and gloomy to just plain tired and cranky.

Chelsea threw herself against her pillow, seemingly disappointed that she hadn't been able to get Alex, or anyone else, stirred up. Then, the twelve girls in 3C went back to whispering about whatever they whispered about when the room was dark.

▲ ▲ ▲

"Final electives!" Julie yelled the next morning. Each girl needed to pick her last two free-choice activities for the very last two weeks at Camp Lakeview.

Only two more weeks! Alex thought. Part of her was happy that it was almost over. She couldn't wait to see her parents and her friends from home again. But part of her was so sad, too.

Alex huddled with Brynn to make the big decision. Brynn was such a drama queen, and Alex preferred to have her drama on a theater or television screen. Even though they were so different, their friendship worked—well, most of the time. Brynn created action and excitement, while Alex kept the two of them on time and grounded. Alex admired Brynn's free spirit. Because of her, Alex rarely got bored.

"I have to take drama, of course," Brynn said. "Then I think I'll take nature."

"I have to take sports, of course," Alex answered, laughing. "Then I'll take . . . it's a secret."

"Tell me!" Brynn begged. "Best friends tell each other everything."

"It won't be a secret if I tell you," Alex said, poking and tickling Brynn so she wouldn't get mad at her for not telling.

"Puh-*leeeeeease!?*" Brynn said, this time using the full range of her booming voice. Alex couldn't help it. She caved.

"Okay, okay. Is there any chance I could talk you into taking ceramics with me? Puh-*leeeeeease!?!*" Alex added, making Brynn laugh again. She wished she and Brynn could finally have an activity together. After all, there was no way Alex could take drama—she considered herself allergic to the stage spotlight. She preferred to shine on the soccer field.

"Just take drama with me," Brynn said. "I'll help you! It would be so cool. You never know—you might be a star."

"No," Alex answered, knowing full well that she might as well be in drama since she'd be helping Brynn with her lines like she always did. That's how it had always been between the two friends. "No, no, and no," Alex added. "Come on, do ceramics this once."

"I love you, Alex, but you can't ask me to give up my whole entire life for you," Brynn said, kind of teasing, kind of not.

Alex sighed. "All right," she said. There was no point in trying to change her mind. Brynn was just excited for her big play after all—this year's production of *Peter Pan* was going to be a blast!

The other girls from the bunk flocked to Julie's sign-up clipboard. Julie was always smiling, and everyone loved her. It didn't even bother her to get bum-rushed by a gaggle of excited girls. While Alex waited patiently for the mob to clear, she heard Jenna ask to be in photography with her brother Adam again. Alex was happy to see they were getting along better. Jenna'd had a rough spot a few weeks ago when she pulled a crazy prank, letting all of the animals free to howl and poop and cry during the camp social. Jenna had temporarily lost her brain, but thankfully, it seemed to have found its way back into her head. Grace and Brynn signed up for drama, and they vowed to be partners so Grace wouldn't end up with a bully like Gaby again. Natalie and Alyssa asked to be on the newspaper together, and Val, always the independent one, signed up for woodworking.

"You just want to be with the boys!" Chelsea teased Val. The boys were a divisive issue for some of the girls. Jenna and Alex were on the anti-boy, anti-flirting side, while some of the others were starting to have crushes. Alex couldn't understand why boys were so important. Her friends were talking about them, walking around with them, and worrying about what they did or didn't do. Alex thought it was just easier to be friends with them— just friends—so they didn't take any time away from her already jam-packed life. She had a lot of guy friends—she loved playing soccer with Theodore Cantor and Andre Derstein back home—but that didn't mean she wanted to *hold hands* with either of them. In fact, the idea creeped her out. Alex figured she was lucky she felt that way. Her parents were so conservative that she knew she wouldn't be allowed to date until she was at least thirty.

"Oh, yeah, the boys," Valerie said. "I'm not stupid," she added, flipping her long cornrows into Chelsea's face. Alex knew that Val was just playing along, though. Val was really good at woodworking, whether half the boys happened to be in that class or not. She'd already made a cutting board, a lamp, and a carved plaque with an elephant on it that hung on her bunk. Valerie had the funkiest jewelry and decorations and clothes. Alex was always admiring her stuff in their bunk. She felt like her own choice of decor—plain navy sheets that matched her mostly navy and white outfits—were getting totally boring.

Thinking about trying new, artsy things, Alex got excited again. She had told Grace that arts and crafts were smelly and boring just a few weeks ago, but she didn't feel that way anymore. It was time to try something other than sports. Alex had been inspired by the Ninja Supertwins book she was reading—one of the twins is an awesome sculptor—and by her friend Bridgette from home who had signed up for painting class at the local art museum. Alex had been in a funk lately—she hoped a change of pace would help. So when the other girls had made their picks, Alex made her move.

"Here comes young Mia Hamm," Julie said, making Alex smile, not to mention blush. "So, what'll it be?"

"Ceramics, please," she answered, moving her knapsack—the one she *always* carried—to the opposite shoulder. Alex had seen the necklaces some girls had made in the last session. They were these shiny, round beads that hung from a leather strap. Alex knew her mother, an art teacher, would love to have one. Her mother would be so happy to get a necklace from Alex, too, since Alex was rarely interested in noncompetitive activities. Alex had always known she was a little bit more like her dad, a litigations lawyer who lived for trials that put the bad guys in jail.

"You want ceramics?" Julie asked, totally surprised. She'd known Alex for years, and when she put Alex in arts and crafts three years ago, Alex had cried. (Alex was still embarrassed about that, but she figured she was only eight years old then!)

"Hey, I may be an old dog," Alex started, "but I can still learn a few new tricks."

"I think that's so awesome of you!" Julie said, paying

close attention to how Alex felt. Julie always paid close attention to everyone, and that's what made her so special. Julie could have five girls screaming in her ear all at once, and each girl would still know that Julie was listening to her. Alex saw Julie as a role model. She could totally see herself becoming a counselor at Lakeview one day.

"Wait, um, Alex," Julie called a few seconds later. "Could you please do me a favor?"

"Sure, anything," Alex said. Julie's face was wrinkled and unsmiling, and that made Alex worry.

"I can't believe I have to tell you this, but . . . hmmm . . . ceramics is full, and I would've saved you a spot, but I just didn't have a clue you'd pick an arts activity," Julie said. "I feel so bad about this, Alex."

"Um, well," Alex replied, her hopes sinking into the hungry part of her stomach. "Okay," she added. She mentally kicked herself for not putting ceramics on her free-choice list that Julie kept earlier. *It's my own fault,* she thought. It seemed like she was always missing out on things because she just didn't speak up in time. She could've been the captain of her soccer team back home—she was the best player on her fifth-grade team—if she had just said that she was interested. She hadn't, so one of her teammates got the role.

"But I can put you in woodworking," Julie said.

Alex's faced dropped. She imagined splinters and nails and difficult projects—and way too many boys. Julie patted Alex's back and started to smile.

"Come on," Julie said. "It's so creative. It really is. You can still try new things in there. I absolutely promise that you will have fun."

"Do I have any other choice?" Alex asked.

"Um, well," Julie said carefully, "not really, sweetie."

"Okay, okay," Alex answered, sensing that Julie was about to be disappointed in her.

"Sweetie, you are *the best*," Julie said, hugging Alex. "I can always count on Camp Lakeview's very own Mia Hamm. Don't you worry, either. There's a really nice instructor in there, and you're always a star at everything you do."

Alex smiled a little bit, even though she was disappointed. When it came down to it, she loved making other people happy, especially Julie. Alex just wished that something would start going her way. She didn't understand why she was feeling so sad.

chapter

TWO

When Alex was on the soccer field, there was no Chelsea to antagonize her. There were no free-choice mishaps. There was no Brynn overdramatizing about her drama class. There were no cranky campmates. There was, for once, only Alex. And she was the star.

She had been looking forward to the afternoon because that day, for their usual post-breakfast bunk activity, her mates were taking on their rivals, the girls from 3A. Both bunks had chosen to play soccer.

When the announcement was made, Alex felt like finally she would have a good day, and she was right.

As usual, she had been chosen as the leader of her 3C team, and that made her feel confident. She wasn't the fastest runner—Sarah had that strength. She also wasn't the strongest goalie—Jenna could make that claim. But Alex *was* the most fearless player. The ball was her pet. Alex could skillfully follow it, volley it, chase it, and kick it as if it were attached to her Diadora soccer cleats. The soccer ball met its match every time Alex took to the field.

But the other team, the girls from bunk 3A,

were playing a really good game. Alex wanted to win, and the score was six for her team, eight for the enemies, er, opponents. She started to freak out. Alex would rather lick bugs every day for two weeks than lose a game of soccer.

She thought of her favorite childhood book, *The Little Engine That Could*. She knew it was silly, but that story—one her mother had read to her once a week from nursery school through the first grade—always got her spirits up. She'd tell herself *I think I can, I think I can* whenever she got nervous before a test or game or meeting with a teacher. Then during whatever made her nervous, she'd change the words to *I know I can, I know I can*.

Today, with the other team's score creeping up, she added another line to the cheerleader in her head. She thought, *I know I can. I know we can. I know, I know, I know.* She didn't like to brag or anything—bragging was bad manners according to Alex—but she had to get herself psyched to win three more points and take the game. As the next time-out happened, she took charge—something she'd been doing a lot this summer—and gave the only advice she knew that would help them win.

"You all are awesome! You are better than these girls! You can kick their tails—I've seen you do it before. Now come on!" she yelled. The girls from 3C just watched her.

Candace said, "We can kick their tails!"

Jessie yelled, "You betcha!"

Others stood in the huddle with their mouths open. Some were really passionate about soccer, but most just saw it as a way to have some fun. Those who weren't as competitive were the ones Alex had to get pumped up.

"My shins are getting sore," Alyssa said, bending

over to rub them.

"My throat hurts," Chelsea whined, twirling her hair around her pointer finger.

That's when Valerie stepped in, "You all are fine. You have to be! We're gonna win!" Valerie was always like that—she had the sunniest attitude of anybody. Alex was starting to realize that Val was never, ever in a bad mood.

"That's right, we are," Jenna added with pursed lips and furrowed brows. She took soccer as seriously as Alex did.

"Who's the best?!" Alex yelled, relieved that the whiners—there were always two or three on every team—had been shut down. She was even more relieved that Valerie had been the one to do it. She was such a cool girl. No one could argue with Valerie.

"Um, you are," Natalie answered, looking at Alex.

"No!" Alex laughed. "*We* are!"

After the pep talk, Alex started talking strategy. She told Sarah to run past the other team's best runner— that would distract her from the game at hand. Jenna had three girls to cover. Brynn was supposed to stand near the goal and block anyone who came toward Alex when she went in for the point. Even the whiners came on board for the winning plans.

By the end of the time-out, no one was unmotivated anymore. Instead, their expressions were determined. The girls looked like they took this game seriously, and even better, they looked like they wanted to win.

They huddled up in a circle like a bunch of NFL football stars and yelled their bunk cheer, "We be 3C!" It wasn't poetry, but it was catchy. They high-fived and cheered one another as they ran back to the field.

The other team watched them quietly. Alex could tell her opponents were worried, and she was glad. Her team really did have the edge on the winning mindset, which meant they were halfway there.

Alex was so pumped. She stole the ball from Gaby, wheedled it through the players with ease, and scored. Then she scored again. And again.

Because of Alex's talent and the rest of the crew's enthusiasm, they were able to take the game, and they took it fast. Neither team could even believe what had happened. The girls from 3C, with Alex in the lead, had won. But most surprising was that it hadn't even been very difficult. Alex was proud and happy and confident all at the same time.

Afterward, panting and sweating like happy puppies, the girls congratulated the other sullen-faced team, and then they hugged one another. They clapped and laughed and basked for just a few extra minutes.

Even if they were getting the end-of-the-summer blues at times, everyone really had bonded over the last few weeks. They'd proven it on the soccer field—whenever someone needed support, another girl ran to her rescue. Together, when 3C needed to rally, they could do it.

Alex couldn't have been more pleased—she forgot all of her problems for that second. Nothing else mattered except that she had done her job, and she had done it well.

Of course, that was typical for Alex. Anytime there were tasks to be completed, Alex was always asked to do them. Teachers knew if they needed help grading papers, Alex was their girl. Moms would let their kids stay out later as long as Alex was with them. Friends could count on Alex to help them with their homework or any other problems that they had. Alex just had this way about her of doing the right thing. But she was really hard on herself—she was a total perfectionist.

Alex wasn't judgmental of others, though. She figured that people had their flaws, and those flaws made them unique, even cute. Meanwhile, she beat up on herself. She couldn't remember the last time she'd received a B in school. Anything but an A-plus was unacceptable to her. Report card day always made Alex's parents so happy— they were big on good grades.

It wasn't just school either. At camp, Alex always got up five minutes earlier than everyone else so she could tidy up her stuff after she got ready in the morning. She'd make her navy and white bed and neatly stack toiletries into her cubbyhole. Even her shoes were lined up alongside the foot of her bed. She never went frantic looking for a lost flip-flop or barrette like Brynn did. Alex never left her room—or her bunk—unless everything was in order. She was always on time (even though she was always sneaking off to take care of a secret personal errand) and during the school year, she always carried around her to-do list.

Alex's mom thought she put too much pressure on herself. She was always giving Alex those relaxing CDs where frogs chirp and water gurgles. Alex knew she should try to take it easy, but it just didn't seem like she was built that way. She hadn't even ripped open the plastic on those calming CDs that were tucked away deep in her summer suitcase.

"It's too bad you're too young to be Color War captain," Jenna said as they headed back to the bunk to get cleaned up for dinner.

"Really? You think I'd be a good captain?" Alex asked, surprised.

"Duh!" Jenna yelled, rolling her eyes.

"But Jenna, you're really good at soccer, too," Alex said.

"I just have to admit that you're better," Jenna added. "I wish I could be captain—it would be so cool—but I was watching you out there. You've just got *it*."

Alex could feel her heart beating fast, her body getting excited. She tried not to smile too much—she didn't want to be braggy—but she almost couldn't help it. "Got what?" Alex asked.

"*It!*" Jenna and Brynn yelled at the same time.

That was a big thing for Jenna to say. She had been upset when Alex had turned out to be a better diver a few weeks ago. Alex did everything she could to help Jenna with diving—even spent time with her at the lake—but Jenna just kept getting more and more upset when she couldn't do it right. They worked it out, though, and Jenna even improved her diving.

Alex understood that Jenna could be really competitive. That's why it was especially nice for her to say these things to Alex now. After all, the two of them had been coming to Camp Lakeview together forever. Even though they were close, it always felt like they were rivals, albeit friendly ones.

"Oh stop it, you all," Alex said, hoping that she really would get to be the captain in a few years. She couldn't help but think about how she'd missed being captain of her school soccer team last year.

"You're going to give Alex a big head!" Brynn interrupted, teasing her.

"Nah, we won't," Valerie added, smiling.

"Doesn't that distinction go to Chelsea, anyway?" Grace whispered to Alex.

"Can we stop talking about it, please?" Alex asked, embarrassed by all the attention. She hoped they all meant it—she was thrilled!

Do they think I'm the best at sports? she wondered, smiling.

"Um, okay then," Karen said, and everyone hushed to look at her. Karen rarely spoke out loud. She could only be seen whispering to Chelsea, although lately she'd been standing up for herself more and not letting Chelsea boss her around *quite* so much. "I have a question for Alex. Could you tell me, what's Color War?" Karen said.

Alex liked Karen a lot, even though the girl was a different kind of person. She had about twenty stuffed animals around her bed. Alex understood that some girls still liked their stuffies—but everyone else had only brought one, if that.

"You've got to be kidding me," Chelsea answered, irritation in her voice. She hated when someone else got all the attention.

Alex sidled up to Karen and started telling her all about it—Color War was absolutely Alex's favorite time at camp. "That's when everyone here gets divided up into two groups, Red and Blue. For two whole days, we compete with each other—even with the girls in our own bunk—to see which team will win the Lakeview Champion Title," Alex explained as her heart started beating faster.

"Um, cool," Karen said. Karen wasn't very competitive, so Alex wondered if she really meant it. But at least Karen seemed genuinely interested.

"Most of the competitions are sports," Alex said, "but not all of them. I mean, we do soccer, blob tag, Scrabble, basketball, canoeing, croquet, swimming, and singdown. For the first time all summer, bunkmates could be on separate teams, and best friends could be enemies," she added.

Luckily for Alex, though, she had always managed to be on the same team as Brynn. She couldn't imagine trying to beat out her best friend in anything.

To Alex, Color War was special because, while it tore the camp apart for two days, it also brought everyone closer together at the end. Unlike other camps, at Lakeview, the winners had to do something really nice for the losers—this year, like last, they would have to make chocolate chip cookies. That was always fun because those who make the cookies also get some of the dough, of course. Alex enjoyed the process and the camaraderie and delivering the treats to the other kids at the end of dinner last year. She hoped it would be just as much fun this year—even though she definitely wouldn't be having any treats.

Getting ready for Color War was just as much fun as actually doing it, too. The teams always got together in secret huddles to pick outfits, mascots, and cheers and to make signs and to plan pranks on their opponents. Even though Alex knew the drill by now—she still totally loved Color War at Camp Lakeview.

Last year, Alex, Sarah, and Brynn had been on the winning team together. Because they understood one another so well, they were able to score the last point for their team during a lay-up competition on the basketball court. After a perfect pass from Sarah, Alex threw the ball into the basket while Brynn cheered them on. They were so happy to win for their division that Alex cried a little while everyone yelled and screamed her name. She was sweaty and hugging her best friends, so she didn't think anyone had noticed how emotional she'd been.

It was a special day and a very lucky shot. She went home savoring her victory. She thought last year was the best time she'd ever had away at camp. She didn't think it could get any better.

"You're going to love it," Alex told Karen, who was a first-year. "I hope we get to be on the same team. I'll show you the secrets to winning all the different events."

Karen was so quiet that Alex hadn't gotten to know her very well. She really did hope that the two of them could hang out some more before it was time to pack up and head home in less than two weeks. But Karen was always with Chelsea, though she had been branching out after the incident at the water park. Alex was so glad that Karen wasn't letting Chelsea be so pushy anymore.

"Alex, you don't have to know everything about *everything*," Chelsea said, taking Karen aside to explain Color War to her all over again.

Alex got tingly because she could sense Karen's suffering, and she *so* wanted Karen to tell Chelsea off. Alex kind of understood, though. Sometimes, like just now, Alex didn't speak up, either. Alex had the guts, that wasn't the problem, she just didn't like all the drama that came along with speaking up.

"I, um, was just answering Karen's questions," Alex said, moving away from Chelsea and over to Brynn. Brynn would tell the queen bee where to go if it became necessary. That was one thing about Brynn, no one intimidated her, and she was known to mouth off if someone pushed her buttons.

"You were showing off, Alex," Chelsea added, "and you know it. Karen, don't listen to her. I'll explain it all to you."

"I heard her, Chelsea—" Karen started to say.

Chelsea started in, "Well, first of all, it was pretty stupid to not know what Color War is. I mean, come on. Second, I would've told you, honey, if you'd just asked."

Karen hung her head down toward her feet. She was such an abused puppy most of the time, though she was slowly starting to show some teeth. Alex wondered how Karen got to be so mousy.

"I can't believe you," Brynn said to Chelsea.

Karen's face turned red. She put her head back up, and she said, "It's okay, really. I get it now, and there's no reason to—"

"Sweetie, don't you have lines to read or something? I'm sure Alex can help you learn them since she's so good at everything all the time," Chelsea added, pulling Karen ahead of the group so they would be able to jump into the showers first.

"She needs to take a chill pill," Grace said.

"She should really try meditation," Alyssa added, which came out of nowhere. Alyssa often came out of nowhere, but at least she always had something new—and unique—to say.

"Forget about her, you guys," Valerie said.

"Yeah, we just won an awesome soccer game," Alex

said, not wanting anyone to argue with each other. "So let's just think about that right now."

Natalie and Alyssa ran past Chelsea and Karen, their way of beating Chelsea to the showers. Everyone was really pulling together, even Karen. It made Alex feel good.

THREE

"Hey, come sit with me," Valerie said as Alex entered the woodworking cabin for their second free-choice period. Valerie had arrived late the day before, so they hadn't been able to share a table. "We girls gotta stick together."

"Thanks," Alex said, sitting down and still wishing she had been able to take ceramics class with her other friends. She liked Valerie fine, she just didn't know her that well. But even worse, Alex just didn't give a flying Frisbee about woodworking. She'd never taken shop class in school for a reason—it sounded really boring. She liked to do stuff that had lots of action, like soccer and swimming and running and volleyball. Wood just sat there and did nothing.

"Hey, Alex," Adam, Jenna's twin brother, called.

"What are you doing here? You're supposed to be in photography with your sister," Alex said, dreading the free-choice period ahead.

"I'm here to make your life miserable," he told Alex, tapping his pencil on the girls' table.

"Yes, you are," Alex said.

He was right—he was going to torment her. Alex tolerated him because she'd known him ever since she started coming to Lakeview. But he had been on her last nerves lately. He had teased her after the soccer game, calling her Lanky Legs and Spider Woman. He had also snapped her training bra the other day. That really ticked Alex off. She knew she was too flat-chested to be wearing one in the first place. Her mother made her wear it because Alex played so many sports. (Alex's mom wanted her to be used to bras for when she really needed them, if that made any sense.) And to have Adam flicking the stupid thing was just embarrassing.

Alex had wanted to ask Jenna to tell him to stop, but that only would only have made matters worse. Jenna *and* Adam would be on Alex's case about her training bra. That would be too embarrassing for Alex to handle. Alex thought he should be spending more time with Alyssa, anyway—ever since the social, they seemed to have a sort-of romance brewing.

"I can tell when I'm not wanted," Adam said as he wandered over to the corner where his friends were hanging out. Alex was relieved. She wasn't in the mood to deal with boys very often.

"Alex, did I just see what I thought I saw?" Valerie asked, tossing her long braids behind her back and out of her way.

"What? Adam Spasm?" Alex started calling him that when they were seven years old. That summer, Adam told everyone he had a magic reaction to peas. Whenever that vegetable was served, he'd eat one and start shaking all over uncontrollably. It had been very difficult to eat whenever peas were served. He'd make everyone laugh so hard, they'd shoot food—including peas—out of their mouths and noses.

"Yeah, I'm pretty sure he's into you," Val said, eyeing the stool she was finishing.

Alex's heart started beating so hard that she thought she'd need to go to the infirmary. "You've got to be kidding me," she said louder than she meant to. "Anyway, I mean, he's Adam *Spasm!*" Her face immediately started going hot, and she looked around to make sure no one else could hear what Valerie had just said. Adam was a friend of hers—just a friend. Of all people to have her first crush on, *if* that were ever to happen, it most definitely would never *ever* be him. Because he was Jenna's twin brother, that kind of made him like Alex's brother, too. *Ewww!* Alex thought.

Besides, she wasn't into boys. She didn't like the way other girls were starting to make such a big deal out of them. Natalie was always planning her day so she could hang around with Simon, Chelsea flirted with some boy in an older division, Grace was flirting with Devon from 3F, and even Brynn was starting to get gooey-eyed when a certain boy from drama was around (though she would *never* have admitted that to Alex). Alex could see it happening all around her, and she didn't like it. She could take or leave boys. She didn't spend that much time thinking about them except with they snapped her bra or smelled bad after playing baseball. She had other important things to think about, like soccer. And something that she just couldn't share with anyone.

"Oh stop it, Val," Alex said matter-of-factly. It had only taken half a minute, and she had gotten control of herself once again. She was absolutely shocked and embarrassed to even think about the possibility of Adam liking her. Then she added, "Adam has a thing for Alyssa, anyway. Didn't you see the way they were hanging out at the social? They're practically each other's prom dates already."

"Where've you been, girl?" Val asked, leaning in to whisper to Alex. At least Valerie wasn't like Brynn when it came to sensitive issues. When Brynn was excited, she yelled out whatever was on her mind, and everyone heard all about it. Sometimes Brynn's enthusiasm was endearing; sometimes it was terrifying. But the dramatic outbursts had really been embarrassing Alex lately. Especially when Brynn had started talking about Alex's training bra in front of Chelsea a few nights ago.

"Why? Where do you think I've been?" Alex said, feeling panicked about something other than Adam. Alex thought Valerie had figured it out—sometimes she'd miss swimming or lunch or evening campfires. That's because she was always running an errand, but Alex couldn't tell anyone what that errand was. Alex believed her problem was really gross and embarrassing. So she would just sneak away a few times a day, take care of it, and sneak back. Alex got away with it by telling everyone she was helping Julie or Marissa. That wasn't a stretch, either, because she *was* always doing stuff with them. She just freaked because she thought Val had figured it out.

"Huh? You really haven't heard, have you?" Valerie said, totally oblivious to the mini panic attack Alex just had. "A couple of days ago, Alyssa started hanging out with Simon's good friend Trevor. She just ignores Adam now. He seemed really hurt about it last weekend. Are you sure no one told you?"

"I had no idea! You're kidding!" Alex said, relieved that Valerie hadn't figured out her real secret. All of a sudden, Alex started feeling bad for someone else: Adam. He really was a cool kid, especially for a boy, despite the pea spasms. Alex certainly didn't want him to be depressed about a girl. Adam was always making Jenna feel better when she was down, and he was a volunteer coach for the little kids, too. He'd show them how to throw Wiffle balls and go dog-paddling. He also played soccer sometimes with Alex, which was fun because he was really good. Alex was surprised that Alyssa would be so rude to Adam. But she liked Alyssa, so Alyssa must've had a good reason to start liking Trevor.

"Maybe I should make sure he's doing okay," Alex said, mostly to herself. She thought Adam had been acting weird lately, and that was definitely why. He was heartbroken, and he needed his old friends. She thought she'd ask him to play soccer or something to get his mind off of it.

"I knew you had a thing for him!" Valerie said, getting very excited about this prospect. After all, Alex had never had a crush, and everyone knew it.

"Wait one second," Alex interrupted. "Before you get this all wrong, Adam and I are just friends. He's just feeling bad, and I need to be there for him if he wants to talk or anything. I know he really liked Alyssa. We're like brother and sister, anyway. He knows there is no way on Earth that I'd ever be interested in him. And vice versa!"

"You sure?" Valerie said, completely uninterested in the stepping stool she was making for her dad's garage.

"I'm totally sure. Ewww. I'm just not boy crazy yet, and I don't think I ever will be," Alex added, and she meant it. Other girls said their crushes made their hearts beat faster, distracted their thoughts, and made them want to hold hands and stuff. That just sounded way too complicated for Alex. She didn't understand what they were talking about. She'd never felt that way. Ever. And that was fine with her.

"Me neither, not anymore," Valerie said. "I had a boyfriend in the beginning of the fifth grade, and he transferred out of our school. It broke my heart! Not because we were all lovey-dovey and stuff. But because we were best friends. I missed him! I made close friends with some other girls, though—thank God!"

Alex knew that feeling, her former best friend, Maggie, had moved away in the fourth grade. It wasn't easy getting close to someone else again. It had taken her a year to meet a new best friend at school, a girl named Bridgette. Sometimes Alex really missed her. Bridgette knew Alex better than the girls at camp did. She understood why Alex acted kind of weird sometimes and why Alex had to sneak away. Alex wished she could break down that mystery wall between her bunkmates and herself. She wanted to tell them her secret, but she just couldn't. It was just too awful and embarrassing.

"It's really hard," Alex said. "I'm so sorry you have to go through that."

"It's okay. I'm having a blast this summer," Valerie said, putting down the stool. "Being here makes it easy to forget about how up and down last year was."

"You have a best friend here at least, don't you?" Alex asked. She'd seen Valerie and Sarah together a lot in the beginning of the summer.

"Well, sort of," Valerie said. "But Sarah has been

ignoring me lately, actually. She's been hanging out with Brynn. I'm sure you've noticed that."

That was true, though Alex hadn't thought about it that way. Alex had gotten tired of constantly practicing Brynn's lines for the *Peter Pan* play. So she had been so relieved when Sarah started offering to do it. It gave her so much more time to swim and play soccer, the things Alex lived to do. She hadn't even stopped to think about how Valerie felt about the new Brynn and Sarah twosome.

"You're right, she has," Alex said, worrying that maybe Brynn was starting to like Sarah better. "Don't you hang around with them?"

"Nah, only in the rec hall and stuff. I don't feel right. They have so many inside jokes and stuff lately," Valerie said, grabbing a nail. Alex couldn't get a sense of whether she was upset about it or not.

"You okay?" Alex asked, touching her shoulder. She was usually good at sensing how other kids felt. She was starting to believe Valerie, despite her cheeriness, was getting a little bit lonely. That was a feeling Alex could relate to.

"I'm fine," Valerie said. "Now let me show you how to make a cutting board."

"A cutting board?" Alex asked, once again dreading her commitment to woodworking.

"I know it doesn't sound like much fun, but it's the first thing we all have to make in here. It's because a cutting board is simple, and you have to use a lot of the tools to do one. The project is mostly to get you familiar with the tools, honestly. You can give it to your mom, too. I mean, all moms like to chop up vegetables and try to make us eat them, right?" Valerie asked, getting up from their long metal table.

"Oh, yes!" Alex answered. Her mom was always telling her how important it was to eat broccoli, peppers, carrots, radishes, lettuce, onions, peas, squash, yams, mushrooms, asparagus, artichokes, eggplant, cucumbers, cauliflower, cabbage, zucchini, celery, and Brussels sprouts. Alex's mother was an expert in rabbit food. And, as it turned out, no one ate more rabbit food than Alex. "My mom will totally love this cutting board," Alex said. She was feeling a little better about missing ceramics. If she couldn't make her mother a necklace, at least she could make her something.

They started drawing on the blank slab of wood that Valerie had brought over to Alex. The slab was the size of a laptop or dinner tray. Alex looked at it, wondering what the heck she'd do with it. It was so drab and dull and, well, *woody.*

Valerie had started on her stool again, but with Alex's wide-eyed look of confusion, Valerie pushed her project aside. Alex thought that was really nice. Valerie picked up a pencil and a ruler and started drawing on the slab; she drew a paddle shape and turned it over.

"Now, you try," Valerie said to Alex.

"Why? You already did a good job on the other side," Alex answered. She didn't see why anyone should do the work twice.

"But my cutting board outline was sloppy. I definitely think you could do a better job," Valerie said, trying to appeal to Alex's competitive streak.

Her approach worked. Alex started making the shape, using the eraser to fix any wobbly lines. When she was finished, the shape was perfect.

Valerie told Alex that she had a secret gift for drawing, but Alex insisted that if she could draw, it was only because her mother was an art teacher.

Next, Valerie showed Alex how to use the saw to cut the shape into the slab. They thought the spewing sawdust looked like Chelsea's hair in the morning, and they thought the buzzing noise sounded a whole lot better than Julie's alarm clock. Alex didn't realize that more than thirty minutes had gone by. Finally, Valerie got out a wood plane—kind of like a big nail file—to sand the splinters off the freshly cut board. Alex used the tool to rub the rough edges until they became smooth, and it *was* just like filing her nails into the perfect short shape she liked to keep them in. Another twenty minutes later, the girls were almost done with the entire cutting board project. The new boys in the class were barely finished drawing theirs.

"Whoa! What, are you two going to start your own carpentry class?" Adam's friend Jack said to them.

"Maybe we will!" Alex laughed. She never dreamed she'd actually enjoy woodworking. Not only that, she was pretty good at it. She was petite, but also very strong. That meant she could hold the wood against the noisy, gigantic saw that chopped it into usable pieces. Her arms didn't get tired when she was sanding with the wood plane either—back and forth, back and forth, smoothing all the edges. Tomorrow, she was going to stain it a reddish brown color to go with her mother's dishes. It wouldn't look plain or boring at all when she was done with it. She was shocked at how excited she was to start making her next project.

She was also excited because Valerie had been so

much fun to partner with. Alex usually spent all of her free time with Brynn, and she realized that she might've been missing out on getting to know other cool girls. Valerie was so helpful, and she didn't complain once. Nor did she ask Alex to do anything for her. She didn't bring up the Adam thing anymore either—Val seemed to have that sixth sense of when to drop things. Alex thought that she and Val just *got* each other. They laughed at the same jokes, they never ran out of things to say, and neither one of them wanted to flirt with all the boys who kept teasing them. Yes, Alex was feeling much, much better about woodworking. The last two weeks of her time at Camp Lakeview might even be a whole lot better than she imagined.

chapter

FOUR

The next day, Alex spotted Adam drinking orange juice at the table right behind her at breakfast. He kept poking Jenna, trying to tell her something. Alex couldn't help but notice, now that Valerie had said something, that he did seem to be hanging around all the time. She'd seen him at meals in the rec room, in woodworking, and out on the soccer field. But Jenna had been eating and playing soccer with Alex, so Adam was probably just spending more time with his sister because *part* of what Valerie had said was totally true. Alyssa had been buddy-buddy with Simon's friend Trevor a whole bunch of times. Alex figured Adam was probably upset about it. She imagined that no one, boy or girl, would enjoy getting dumped.

It worked out really well for Alyssa—too well as far as Alex was concerned. She couldn't help but think it: Alyssa got together with Trevor so she could spend a lot more time with Natalie and Simon. Simon *was* pretty much Natalie's boyfriend. It was really weird how things worked out, and the whole incident just confirmed for Alex how strange her friends started acting once they became interested in boys. Alex thought camp (and school, for that matter) would be a lot more fun if the boys and girls just stayed friends and stopped flirting so much. Alex knew she sure wasn't flirting with anyone. She thought she might even talk to her parents about going to an all-girl high school one day.

"So, I have this idea," Valerie said, hopping onto her stool at their table later that day during woodworking. Valerie was always a few minutes late for class because she was a free spirit. Alex was used to it—no one she knew was as prompt as she was. When Valerie finally arrived, Adam scurried away from the girls' table. Thankfully, Valerie didn't say anything about the situation—surely, she thought Adam was flirting with Alex again. Valerie was so wrong about her theory. Alex and Adam were just good friends!

"You like to play chess, right?" Valerie asked Alex, unpacking her woodworking supplies. Valerie just figured that Alex was super smart. A few weeks ago, when Grace had to read *Call of the Wild* because she had fallen behind in her fifth-grade reading class, Alex was the one who had helped her the most. Alex had read the book two times— for fun. In fact, Valerie guessed that some of the other girls, mainly Chelsea, were even jealous of Alex because she was smart in addition to being athletic and well-liked. This thought made Valerie excited for one reason in particular: because really smart people knew how to play chess.

"Actually, I don't," Alex answered, standing next to the metal table in the woodshop. She had come into class with her soccer ball in her hands, and the instructor— a nice college student named Jeremy (a guy who really needed to take the tape off the bridge of his glasses)—had taken it away from her. He wasn't worried that Alex and Valerie would cause trouble or break things. Instead, he didn't want the boys in the class to start a game of keep-away right there in the cabin. They were kind of wild sometimes, especially Adam Spasm and his friends.

"Oh well," Valerie said, twisting her long black braids and slumping a little on the stool. Valerie was always sitting. Alex always stood.

"Do you play?" Alex asked, putting her hair in a ponytail with the rubber band that was around her wrist. She wished she had a mirror, so it wouldn't look so crooked.

"Yeah, but not here this summer. No one knows how to!" Valerie said. "It's okay." She started getting all the tools together for her next project.

"Wait, I've always wanted to learn to play," Alex said, following Valerie to the supply closet. Alex was telling the truth, too. She'd seen people—all ages and races—playing chess in the park last Christmas when her parents took her to New York City. They were competing on concrete tables outside in the cold—and it was *really* cold in New York in December. Those chess players had the kind of dedication Alex could admire. She asked her parents to teach her, but they didn't know how either. At home, they usually played GoStop, a Korean card game that was totally fun.

"Will you show me how?" Alex asked.

"You can't be serious," Valerie said, staring at her bug-eyed.

"Oh, I'm serious," Alex said, sneaking a peek at Adam across the room. She just didn't get why girls *like-*

liked boys so much. He was cute, but he was teaching his friends how to spit really long saliva wads and then suck them back into their mouths. She wondered if Simon did stuff like that when his friends were around and if Natalie would still like him if she saw.

"I'd love to!" Alex added. "I mean it!"

The girls made a plan to get together in the rec room after dinner for serious chess lessons. Valerie told Alex that it might take a few nights for her to pick it up. But then Valerie thought of how fast Alex had learned woodworking. She secretly hoped that they could start playing in two nights because, after all, Alex was really smart.

"So what's your idea?" Alex asked.

"Oh, it's no big deal," Valerie said. "I just noticed that the chess set in the rec room is plastic. And it's all beat-up. My dad always plays with me on this really nice marble set we have at home. I thought it would be really cool if we made one in here to keep at Lakeview."

"That's an amazing idea!" Alex said. She loved doing that kind of stuff. She was always helping the counselors with whatever they needed—and anyone else. Why not help the camp? Maybe they could even carve their initials on the bottom with a dedication. It was the least she could do to give back to Camp Lakeview. And it would be fun to play on "her" board year after year, she thought. The only worry Alex had was that chess would be really difficult to learn. *It will be okay. Val will help.*

"I'm just glad you're into it," Valerie added, walking over to ask Jeremy how the heck they were going to pull off this project. "Because carving out all of those little pieces would take me forever by myself."

The two girls laughed a long time before they got to work. They figured out the dimensions of their board and pieces, and they made a to-do list so they'd be able to get it all done during those last two weeks of camp—or hopefully even earlier. Alex and Valerie were concentrating so intently on this idea that they didn't even notice when everyone else left the room for their swimming period.

"Girls," Jeremy said, "if you don't go now, I'll have to lock you up in here."

"Okay. We'll be fine, Jeremy," Alex said to their instructor while Valerie started gathering their stuff.

"She's not kidding, either," Valerie said, giggling. Alex was still working away.

"I'm glad to see such enthusiasm," he said. "But I was kidding. I missed lunch, and I'm starving!"

"And we have to swim. Come on, Alex, let's go to the lake!"

Alex looked up. "Huh?" she said.

"Class is over. Let's hit the water," Valerie said, now gathering Alex's stuff, too.

They ran to the bunk, threw on swimming suits, and headed out to the diving board. Alex didn't even run her post-free period errand that she usually ran. She was in too big of a hurry. She was having too much of an amazing time with Valerie. Plus, her mind was on the chess set, and she just wasn't being her usual organized, on-time, strictly scheduled self.

"Let's be swim buddies," Valerie said, leading the way toward the blue, or more advanced, section.

That's when Alex's memory kicked back in. She suddenly realized that Brynn was probably standing around the corner waiting for her. But it was too late. Alex and Valerie had already dashed to the end of the dock, and they were all set to hurl themselves into the water. Before her plunge, Alex thought that Brynn would be okay since she had been swimming with Sarah for the past two days. At least Brynn wasn't alone, and she probably didn't even remember that Alex was supposed to meet her since she and Sarah had been so tight lately. Alex thought to herself, *Brynn is really cool—she'll totally understand.* After all, Brynn was always losing her camp projects and scripts and keys and swimsuits and socks, and Alex was always helping her find them. Surely, Brynn would understand this one time Alex when just happened to space out.

"Hey, what's wrong?" Valerie said as she looked from the diving board into the water way down below.

"Oh, nothing," Alex said. She didn't want to worry Valerie with any of it, especially if Sarah had been dissing Valerie for Brynn lately. *What a mess!* Alex thought. *Are Sarah and Brynn becoming best camp friends? I don't understand why everyone can't just have fun together.*

"So, partners?" Valerie asked, getting antsy to just get into the water already.

"Sure," Alex said, knowing deep down that Brynn probably would be upset no matter what excuses Alex came up with. Alex decided to hope for the best, and off the diving board they went, the two of them at one time, even though they were not supposed to do that. Their bodies plunged through the twelve feet between the diving platform and the water. After six more seconds, their heads bobbed back up to the top. Alex and Valerie were laughing and splashing each other so much that they didn't even hear the lifeguard blow the whistle.

"Girls, girls!" the lifeguard called. "We can't have

that. One at a time, you know that."

They ran off before they could cause any more mischief. They went to the nearby swimming area where the rest of their friends were sure to be. By the shore, Natalie was lying on a blanket reading her magazines like always. Alyssa was right beside her. Alyssa was so funky and cool, Alex couldn't believe she'd just go and dump Adam like that for Trevor. But Alex would never get involved or say anything to either of them about it—she stayed out of other people's business. Alex decided not to join them and headed toward the lake.

"Hey, Alex," Natalie said. "Hey, Valerie."

Valerie stayed by the blanket to talk for a while. Alex smiled at everyone and said she had to go say hello to Brynn. She and Sarah were floating ten feet off the shore on two separate rafts. Alex swam out to them—assuming she could triple-up with them as a buddy—and gave Brynn a small, playful splash. She acted like nothing had happened, took a gulp, and hoped for the best.

"Ow!" Brynn yelled. "You just got water right in my eye. Geez!"

Alex's stomach dropped. She had been right all along—Brynn was annoyed.

"What were you guys laughing about?" Alex asked, starting to feel sick to her stomach.

"Nothing," Brynn answered, not even looking at her best friend. "You wouldn't get it, anyway."

"Yes, I would!" Alex said back to her. And she did get Brynn's jokes—better than anyone else did, for that matter—and Brynn knew it, too.

"Well, maybe if you had bothered to meet me like you said you would," Brynn added, "I would've told you."

Sarah paddled a discrete few feet away. But Alex was sure Sarah was in hearing distance. She didn't swim *that* far away.

"You know, that was just so incredibly rude," Brynn said to Alex. She was still on the raft, and she used her toes to flick water in Alex's face. "Sarah wouldn't do anything like that to me."

When Alex looked over to Sarah, Sarah looked away. *She heard the whole thing!* Alex thought.

That really ticked Alex off—she hated for other people to be involved in her and Brynn's business. Besides, she and Sarah weren't close or anything, but they had been friends for the past two years. Sarah was quiet and proper, but still competitive. Alex figured she was from a really wealthy family because her parents had houses in Maine, New York, and Florida. And Alex didn't know anyone else with more than one home. Sarah could sometimes be aloof, but she had the best manners—she always congratulated the losing team and asked politely for Alex's untouched desserts.

Alex had never seen Sarah cry or yell or even get upset. Her even temper was why they played so well together. But now what would she think of Alex? Alex wished she weren't the kind of person who cared what other people thought of her. But she was.

"Brynn, I didn't mean to! I was having such a good time in woodworking, and I stayed in class too long. Then I ran and got my swimming stuff, and everyone was already out here. I just wanted to jump off the diving board so bad before I got here," she said, pleading with Brynn.

"Yeah, with *Valerie*," Brynn said sarcastically.

"What's wrong with Valerie?" Alex asked. "I didn't

know her too well, but she's super cool. You would think so, too!"

"I can't think about that right now. Do you know that this kind of stress—you blowing me off—is going to make me forget my lines? I'm rehearsing twice a day now—it's so hard. The play is in just over a week! Do you even care?" Brynn asked, now looking at Alex with teary eyes. Alex couldn't believe being swimming partners—or not—was that big of a deal. She and Brynn had met almost every day for free swim for weeks on end. It couldn't hurt them to hang out with other girls. Surely, Brynn understood that she was still Alex's best friend even if Alex did have a lot of fun with other girls sometimes. Like Alex and Jenna—they often took walks together after dinner at night, something Brynn would never want to do.

"Do you only care about the play?" Alex asked. Brynn was being bratty no matter how wrong Alex had been. Alex started to get a sick feeling in her stomach, and she thought that maybe that moment wasn't the best time to pick a fight with her best friend.

"I can't believe you!" Brynn said. "It's not like *I* was the one who did anything wrong!"

All of a sudden, Alex got so dizzy that her heart started to beat fifty times too fast. She was really scared. She could just imagine passing out in the water where she might drown or something.

She was so terrified of getting hurt that she forgot all about Brynn for a second. Her head started to fall backward, and she grabbed Brynn's raft to help balance herself. The dizzy feeling went away, but Alex knew it would be back soon, and she pointed her body toward the shore.

"What are you doing?" Brynn asked, pulling her raft out of Alex's reach.

"I, I'm not feeling so good. Just give me a second," Alex said. She moved her body toward the shore, wobbling all over, and tried to get to her knapsack. She reached inside, grabbed the Tums-like tablet and started chewing it. She plopped her bottom down on the ground and put her head between her legs.

▲ ▲ ▲

"You okay?" Valerie said, running over to where Alex had squatted, underneath a tree and away from the rest of the group.

"Oh, I'm fine," Alex answered, her wobbliness going away. She looked up at Valerie's concerned eyes.

"I'm so sorry I let you go out there by yourself," Valerie said. "I guess that's why we're supposed to swim in pairs. You just never know what's going to happen. Did you see a shark or something?"

Valerie was just joking—everyone pretended there were great whites and barracudas and Loch Ness monsters in the clear, creature-free waters at Camp Lakeview. Alex felt her dizziness going away, and she started laughing. It felt really good to laugh—Alex had been so freaked out just a few seconds before. She really did think she was going to pass out!

Brynn came to the shore and stood next to Alex and Valerie. She saw the two girls talking and then exploded. "I cannot believe you, Alex Kim! You are just so completely overdramatic! Why can't you just face me out there without the act?"

"What act?" Alex answered, wondering which one

of them was the drama queen.

"You know what act—you're playing sick to avoid a fight. You know you'll do anything to avoid a fight, Alex," Brynn said, stomping away.

Alex felt too weak to run after her. She really wanted to tell Brynn she was sorry, and she also needed to know why Brynn was making such a big deal out of everything. Maybe something else was bothering Brynn, or else she was just having a really cruddy day.

"What's got her?" Valerie asked, watching Brynn run off.

Alex shrugged her shoulders, worried that Brynn was super mad at her. Alex just hated big old arguments, and she didn't understand why they couldn't just enjoy the last couple weeks of camp together. She and Brynn wouldn't see each other very much during the year, after all. But then again, Alex was starting to feel like she didn't know Brynn as well anymore.

"Probably the same thing that's gotten a hold of Sarah in the last week," Valerie answered.

"What's that?" Alex asked, feeling better and better.

"Well, I think I accidentally made her mad," Valerie said, scooping up the muddy lakeside sand in her hands and squishing it through her fingers. "I told her that I really missed my crew back home, and I couldn't wait to see them when camp was over in two weeks. See, I have these friends Rachel and Shelly from school, and we've been writing a lot of letters this summer, and I just said that I wished they were here. I didn't mean to make Sarah feel bad at all, but she got up from the table and stomped off. Things have been weird between us ever since."

"No way—you could never make anyone mad," Alex said.

"I guess I was a little insensitive, but Sarah . . . you know, it's kind of hard to get her to open up," Valerie explained. "She doesn't share things with me—she keeps secrets, and that's fine. I mean, I love her—she's awesome. I just wish I hadn't said anything."

"Ohhh, that sucks. So that's why she's been buddy-buddy with Brynn?" Alex asked, feeling less alone.

"I guess so. I can't think of any other reason," Val said. Alex noticed how sad she seemed.

"They'll get over it," Alex said. "I hope." *Why don't Brynn and I see things the same way anymore?* she thought.

"Maybe the mysterious Loch Ness monster ate their brains," Valerie joked.

"Or a shark," Alex answered.

They both laughed, but not for real. They were feeling bad about their friends, or former friends, whatever the case was. They sat together silently for the longest time, just thinking.

chapter
FIVE

For the entire rest of the day, Brynn acted like Alex didn't exist. They usually hung out in between their activities and they almost always walked to dinner together.

But Brynn was nowhere to be found at their usual meet-up times. Alex thought that was really strange. If Brynn was mad, she didn't usually have any trouble telling Alex all about it. In fact, Alex dreaded seeing her because Brynn was sure to chew her out.

As it turned out, though, not talking it out actually made Alex feel worse than a confrontation would have. Alex couldn't shake that awkward, uneasy feeling that something was very, very wrong.

She wondered where her best friend had sneaked off to all day, and while she was upset, she also just hoped that Brynn was okay. Alex had not meant to blow her off as swim partners, and she would tell Brynn she was sorry if she ever got the chance. Alex looked for Brynn everywhere—in the rec room, in the woods by the bunk, in the drama hut, but she still couldn't find her.

At dinner, finally, the two girls were together

again. Alex didn't know if she should go sit next to Brynn at their table in the mess hall. Brynn was with Sarah, and they were giggling and being loud.

Nervous, Alex plopped down next to them. She decided that would be the right thing to do. Alex took a deep breath and got ready to apologize. Even if Brynn had been a little hard on her, it was just easier for Alex to say she was sorry and end the disagreement. Alex had no problem making the first move, and she wanted the uneasiness to go away.

"Hey," Alex said, smiling.

"Hey," Brynn answered back, not smiling at all.

"Are you still mad about earlier?" Alex asked her while she fiddled around with her napkin.

"I'm over it," Brynn said, rolling her eyes and acting sarcastic. "I mean, really, it's not that big of a deal."

"Oh." Alex was surprised that she didn't get chewed out again. "Because I really didn't mean to—" she started to say.

"It's okay, really. Where's Valerie?" Brynn asked.

"She's coming," Alex answered, feeling awkward about the subject of Valerie.

"Great," Sarah added, rolling her eyes. She was turning out to be a lot more competitive than Alex thought!

"I really think we should all just hang out. It would be fun!" Alex said. It seemed like she was always the one rallying and trying to bring everyone together.

Before they could finish their nonconversation, Valerie arrived, asking if she could sit down with them. Sarah and Brynn shrugged their shoulders in unison, their way of saying "whatever" and started talking super-quietly to each other.

The situation didn't feel any less awkward than it had before Alex tried to be nice. In fact, Alex thought things were getting worse. But since she felt like Brynn was shafting her, she just turned to Valerie, and they talked about their chess set and swimming and the boys who had been teaching one another how to spit in woodworking. They ended up making the best of the situation, and dinner wasn't so bad.

Jenna really helped the situation—she told jokes so goofy that mashed potatoes actually oozed out of Candace's nose. Marissa, who served Pete's poor excuse for food, almost spilled a tray, she was laughing so hard when Jenna told the one about the hippopotamus that rode a bicycle through Weehawken, New Jersey. Marissa was laughing so hard, she had to rush back to the kitchen to calm herself down.

"Hey there."

Julie had been off talking to the camp director, Dr. Steve. Now she sat herself down at the table with all the girls. Relief rushed through Alex's veins. She hoped her counselor had noticed the tension at the table and could help them all to work it out.

"Does anyone have any sparkle lotion I could borrow?" Julie asked, humming a happy little song Alex couldn't make out—it might have been "Somewhere Over the Rainbow." Julie continued, "I can't find Marissa's anywhere, and I don't want her to know that I might have, um, misplaced it."

"I do!" Brynn said, and they started talking about how

Julie needed it for her mystery date this weekend. She had the night off on Saturday, and she clearly couldn't wait.

Counselors weren't really supposed to hook up, but it happened, like in the cases of Marissa and Pete, and Stephanie and Tyler. It was cool that Julie trusted the girls enough to tell them about it. They certainly wouldn't spill her secret to anyone. But they did want to know whom Julie liked—and her lips were zipped on that front. A hookup was exciting news even to Alex, who swore she didn't care about boy-girl gossip.

"So, Alex," Julie said, turning toward her, "can you come see me after dinner in the kitchen? I need to ask you something."

"Sure," Alex answered, as usual.

Alex was always helping Julie or Marissa or Pete, one of the chefs, with something. Sometimes they just needed an extra hand to carry something. Other campers were enlisted every so often, too, but it seemed like Alex did the most, which was fine with her. After all, the counselors had their reasons for keeping her busy and keeping an eye on her. She understood. Heck, she appreciated it.

Out of the corner of her eye, Alex could see Brynn and Sarah getting ready to head back to the bunk with the rest of 3C. Was Brynn going to walk off without even saying good-bye?

Without warning, Brynn turned to her abruptly. "See ya later." And then she was off.

Alex tried to calm herself. At least Brynn was speaking to her. She couldn't keep from smiling when she answered, "Cool."

Hopefully, they'd get along well for the night activity

a scavenger hunt. Alex loved those things—outsmarting everyone, finding stuff, and digging up clues.

At the last one, Alex led her bunkmates to the winning item that only had the clue: "Something that's shiny and red." She talked Natalie into letting go of her *Teen People* magazine, and her team submitted it. Even though she knew the counselors meant for campers to capture a ladybug, they let Alex's creative idea pass.

Alex walked back into the kitchen. Most campers never went back there. But it was okay for Alex to step right in and start doing something—like cleaning or putting dishes away. She loved helping if it meant she got to hang out with the counselors.

"What are you here for today?" Pete asked.

He was always cooking hamster surprises and spaghetti worm dinners.

Alex told him they were good—even the Soupy Dooby Doo they had last night—because he was funny and sweet. No one wanted to hurt Pete's feelings— especially not Marissa, who had to actually smile when she ate the, well, slop.

"Julie asked me for a quick hand," Alex answered, stacking some cups next to the dishwasher out of habit.

"Julie's not here. But are you sure you don't want to scrub some pots?" Pete asked, snapping his towel at Alex's ankles.

"Um, I will if you need me to!" Alex said, jumping out of the way before the wet towel zapped her. She really wanted to be on time for the scavenger hunt. "But not if you hurt me—then I won't!"

"You are too much, Alex Kim," Pete said, stuffing his surfer ponytail into the hairnet he was required to wear when he cooked. If he wasn't a culinary talent, at least he was into cleanliness; Alex gave him that.

"I'm just kidding," Pete added. "Now go find Julie. I think she's outside."

△ △ △

Around the back of the mess hall, Julie was sitting at a picnic table filing her nails. She smiled really big when Alex arrived.

"You okay, Mia Hamm?" Julie asked Alex.

Julie reached for Alex's hand so she could file her nails while they talked. Alex was excited—clearly Julie didn't need Alex to help with anything specific, she just wanted to talk. Of course that probably meant she *had* noticed the problems between Alex and Brynn, but Alex didn't care. Spending time alone with Julie made her feel special.

Alex was double thrilled because she was terrible at doing her own nails. She didn't have patience for sitting still to do girlie stuff like that. The only time she'd had her nails painted all summer was when Brynn had done it for her four weeks ago.

"I'm fine," Alex answered evasively.

"You didn't seem fine today at free swim," Julie said, whizzing across the tips of Alex's fingers with the nail file. "You have to take care of yourself."

"I know. I did try to tell Brynn how I felt," Alex answered, trying to sit super still so her hands wouldn't wiggle.

"Oh, that. I didn't know you were having a problem with Brynn," Julie said. Alex was disappointed—Julie had no clue what was going on.

"Oh, no, not really, it's nothing." Alex didn't want to bother her counselor with her silly friend issues. Julie had other things—like twelve campers and zillions of friends and one crush—to think about!

Surely, all of those things are more important than a pair of jousting best camp friends, Alex thought.

"I hope not. You are such a great twosome. You really take good care of Brynn—like when she almost started a bunk pillow fight after everyone had already fallen asleep last week. You don't know how happy I was that you talked her out of it," Julie said, blowing on Alex's nails. "But more importantly, I just want you to take care of yourself."

"Yeah, I know," Alex added, starting to wiggle and squirm. She didn't like where this conversation was heading. She didn't like sitting still. She loved running around.

"So, what I want to ask you is if you'll help in the kitchen for the formal banquet," Julie said, finishing up Alex's ninth finger.

The formal banquet always took place on the very last night at camp, after the drama group's big end-of-summer play, *Peter Pan*. It was 3C's shining night.

Brynn had the part of a Lost Boy, and Grace got to be Wendy. Brynn had actually been really cool when Grace beat her out for that main role. She seemed really happy to be a Lost Boy, surprisingly, and, *un*surprisingly, was putting a ton of effort into rehearsals, fixing the set, and all kinds of other play-related stuff.

"Sure, of course. I thought I already was," Alex said.

"You are the sweetest, I swear," Julie said. "Anyway, thanks. Natalie, Alyssa and Candace are helping out, too.

The four of you need you to come to the planning meeting tomorrow night with the rest of us counselors. It'll be fun. We're going to play Scrabble and stuff after we figure out the menu and plan the desserts. I always like you to have a say on those things, Alex."

She was so happy to be included in any plans that involved the counselors. Alex definitely wanted to be a CIT in a few years, and she thought she'd be really good at it. She loved organizing as many things as possible. With her newly shaped nails—she had to admit they looked pretty good—Alex went back to the bunk in a great mood.

▲ ▲ ▲

Back at 3C, not even Chelsea could ruin Alex's spirits. She and Brynn would work out their differences; Alex was hopeful. Even if Julie hadn't noticed—or given Alex any advice—Alex knew how strong their friendship really was.

"So, what did Julie want, Alex?" Chelsea asked, getting in her face.

"Oh, I'm going to help with the formal banquet," she answered as Chelsea inspected Alex's nails.

"Me too!" Candace yelled enthusiastically. She was too sweet for her own good, but Alex felt kind of sorry for her, too. Candace never had an original thought—ever. At least Candace was good at telling ghost stories. Apparently, she'd learned them all from her older brother.

"Of course you are, Miss Perfect Alex," Chelsea said. "You're always doing whatever you can to kiss the counselors' butts. Just like Natalie and Alyssa and Candace."

"Please, Chelsea," Natalie said, sitting on her bottom bunk on the other side of the room. "What's your problem?"

Alex was glad Nat had chimed in. She didn't know how to react to Chelsea. Today of all days she really wasn't prepared for extra bunk drama.

"You need to mind your own business," Alex said, once she had regained her composure. She looked Chelsea dead in the eye.

The rest of the girls' mouths hung open. But not Brynn. Brynn didn't stand up for Alex. Alex couldn't believe her supposed best friend didn't have her back. Alex really did start feeling sick to her stomach. She didn't even want to be in the scavenger hunt anymore.

"Don't tell me what to do," Chelsea said while Karen ran up to her and tried to distract her. Karen attempted to make Chelsea sit down by offering to French braid her hair. Chelsea finally did sit down, but that didn't mean she would shut up.

"Then don't get in my face," Alex said, wishing she were the kind of person who could give Chelsea's long blond hair a nice short trim in the middle of the night. She hated that this fight was escalating—but Chelsea had managed to push just the wrong button. And right when Alex had been feeling a little bit better . . .

"Don't be such a drama queen," Chelsea added. "Everyone, just relax. I didn't mean what I said. It was rude."

"You don't say," Alex spat.

"Whatever," Chelsea said, over it and preoccupied with Karen's hairstylings.

Everyone was deadly quiet. After a beat, they tried

to go back to hanging out.

Alex looked up to see Brynn walking toward her. Jenna, Jessie, and Candace perked up, watching.

Alex shot them a meaningful look, and they got the hint to mind their own business. They pretended to be busy reading books—except that Jenna's copy of *Are You There God? It's Me, Margaret* was upside down.

"So, Alex," Brynn said, sitting down next to her. "Sorry about that and all. You know how *Chelsea* is," Brynn added loudly so Chelsea would hear.

Chelsea just gave her—and everyone else—an evil eye.

"It's nothing," Alex answered, even though comments like that were everything to her. She was glad that Brynn had at least noticed how hurt Alex had been.

"So, are we on for tomorrow night then?" Brynn asked, sitting down next to Alex on her bed like she always did.

Alex's throat got tight again. *I can't believe what I did!* She had just promised to be at Julie's banquet planning meeting! She wanted to be at that meeting with all the counselors. She wanted to help plan the big dinner and play Scrabble with them afterward! But she had promised to help Brynn paint the *Peter Pan* set for the big show tomorrow night.

Ugh, Alex thought. *How did things ever get so complicated?* She had double-booked, and she couldn't have picked a worse time to do it. Brynn had just started acting like she wasn't mad anymore! Apparently, she hadn't been completely unaffected by Alex's clash with Chelsea. That, at least, was something, Alex thought. Though it didn't exactly solve the current problem.

"So, we are, right?" Brynn said, looking at Alex with her puppy eyes. "I really hoped you could help us."

Alex was no good at painting. She kind of hated it, too. Her mother had made her do way too much of it when she was a little kid. She had only told Brynn she would do it to be nice. She was, however, good at Scrabble. She did like organizing the formal banquet. She would get a say in the menu, and that would be awesome, too.

"Brynn, please don't be mad at me, but I told Julie I'd be at a banquet-planning meeting tomorrow night," Alex said, wishing she had brought her pocket organizer to camp.

"You've got to be kidding me," Brynn said, her voice getting louder and louder. "After today with the swimming and everything?" Brynn stood up, a sure sign that big time theatrics were on the way.

"Please, just try to understand," Alex said, thinking that she'd rather yank off her ponytail at the roots than endure her third fight of the day.

"Understand what?" Brynn yelled, acting like she'd yank out Alex's ponytail for her. "What? That you'd rather hang out with Valerie and Julie and whoever else than with me? I get it just fine."

"I think we need to talk about this. This is not how best friends are supposed to act," Alex said, trying to keep her voice steady.

"Oh yeah, like you're the poster girl for how to be a best friend," Brynn said again, getting all evil-eyed. "Kind of like you were earlier today?"

"You need to get a grip, you are so totally blowing this out of proportion!" Alex yelled. Immediately, she wished she'd just counted to ten first. She knew it was always better to chill out—but Brynn was making that so hard to do!

"Ladies, back to your corners," Grace said, trying to ease the tension with a joke.

"*Grace!*" Alex and Brynn shouted in unison.

All eyes were back on Alex for the second time in five minutes. She'd had the most up-and-down day of anyone at camp. She had never been in this many fights with Brynn—or anyone else—before. Jenna and Alex clashed sometimes, but they always worked it out. They never yelled, either.

Alex really didn't know what to do. Arguing was not her style, and she just wasn't used to it. She felt herself mentally checking out of the situation. She just wanted to run out into the woods—and run and run and run. She couldn't make Brynn happy, and she was tired of trying.

"I don't want your help, anyway!" Brynn yelled as the other girls started to whisper about the impending altercation. When Chelsea chewed out Alex, it was easy for everyone to take Alex's side.

But the fight between Alex and Brynn wasn't so clear-cut. Both girls had a point: Alex was standing Brynn up, and Brynn was being self-involved, not to mention bossy. The other girls—Natalie, Alyssa, Karen, and the others—didn't know what to do. They just looked at one another and shrugged.

Only Sarah and Valerie got involved.

"I'll help you, Brynn," Sarah said, moving to stand next to Brynn.

"Come on, Alex," Valerie said. "Cool down for a while, and then try to talk about it again."

Alex wanted to add one more thing before Brynn walked away. "If Sarah helps, then it's okay if I go to the meeting with Julie?" At least she knew Brynn would have an extra hand, which was the important part, anyway.

"*I said*, I didn't want your help, anyway," Brynn stated, stomping off.

What has Brynn done for me *lately?* Alex wondered. Brynn hadn't even said anything to Chelsea when she harassed Alex just before. Alex honestly didn't think she should be the one to apologize this time.

"It's okay, Alex. Let's just go the scavenger hunt and forget about it," Valerie said. "It will all blow over soon."

"Yeah. Sure." Alex shrugged, trying to shake off the icky feeling the fight had given her. Valerie had to be right. This couldn't go on forever.

Could it?

chapter
SIX

When the girls returned after the scavenger hunt—they had lost to their rival bunk 3A—no one was in a giddy mood. Before lights-out, Brynn and Alex used to sit around and talk. They'd often share their dreams and secrets and rehash the day. Nothing of the sort happened that night.

Alex hadn't expected it, but it still stung when Brynn took her script over to Grace's bed and started reading.

▲ ▲ ▲

It was getting more and more awful by the day—not just for Alex, but also for the other girls who felt like they were being forced to take sides. The most worrisome thing for Alex was that Chelsea and Brynn had been talking more. Alex was terrified that the two of them would gang up together against her and make the last days at camp one big pile of steaming Hamster Surprise.

This was not how Alex had imagined the end of camp! She was so disappointed. She'd managed to have a little fun—like at the formal banquet planning meeting—but she just couldn't enjoy the other camp activities with Brynn acting like they weren't even friends anymore. Alex started wishing that she had gone to paint with Brynn that night instead of to the planning meeting. *Maybe then nothing would've gotten this bad*, Alex thought. But then another, less quiet voice perked up inside her head.

Why should Brynn always get her way? Alex asked herself, vowing to stand her ground on this one. *It's like she just expects me to go play with her.*

As the days went on, woodworking was a much-needed break once a day from the girls and their dramas. Valerie didn't care much about it. She mentioned a few times that her friendship with Sarah was totally over.

"If she's that sensitive, and if I can't talk about my girls at home, then so be it," Val explained. "My mom says sometimes friendships fade, and you should let them go gracefully. If Sarah wants to dump me over one little stupid comment I made, I guess we weren't that close in the first place. Hmph."

"It still stinks, though," Alex added, feeling totally dumped herself. "I hate the way Brynn ignores me."

"Likewise," Val said. "Did you see the way they were holding hands at the flagpole this morning? I couldn't even giggle about Dr. Steve's mismatched knee socks—did you see he had one blue and one orange on today?—because I was fuming over the way those two are acting."

"He did?" Alex asked, shocked that she hadn't noticed.

"I am not kidding. He did," she answered. Val never said anything nasty about Sarah or Brynn, and Alex knew she must've been steamed to have an outburst like that. Alex tried so hard not to say mean things about people, either—though sometimes she did drop an opinion of Chelsea. Alex wondered if Brynn was talking badly about her. *Oooh, she better not be,* Alex thought.

"I don't know about me and Sarah," Valerie said, "but you and Brynn will make up soon. Maybe Brynn is just wigging out about the play."

"That's true. She always stresses out before performances," Alex said, rolling her eyes. "It's so stupid. I mean, I don't freak before Color War or soccer games." For Alex, it was just the opposite. She was so excited for the activities she was good at that her mood actually improved when the pressure was on.

"I know," Valerie added.

At least, with Valerie, Alex felt like she had someone to talk to who really understood. Valerie was always cracking jokes to make Alex smile when she felt like kicking trees. Alex's feelings about Brynn were so up and down. One second, she'd hate her for causing such a big fight. The next second, Alex missed her as if she were a long-lost member of her family. Alex would have given anything to have Brynn back the way she had been during the earlier part of the summer.

"Nice."

"What?" Alex looked up to see Adam standing over her. He nodded appreciatively at the wood she was sanding. She had to admit that the chess board was really coming along.

Valerie excused herself and went to the bathroom. Alex knew what Val must've been thinking. Val thought Adam would be a good match for Alex, so she left the two of them alone together whenever she got the chance. Alex wanted her to stay, though! Adam was hanging around too much and making her really nervous. It was weird.

"What are you guys working . . ." Alex trailed off, realizing that by the time she could get her thoughts together into a normal speech pattern, Adam was already gone.

She could see, from where she was sitting, that Adam and his friends were making a wooden table. It was simple, just a round slab of wood with a base and a pole to hold it up, but it was beautiful. Camp would be over soon, and the boys were working hard to get finished. They were sanding down their project and starting to stain the pieces. They hadn't practiced spitting or tried to steal her soccer ball for three whole days. It was nice when boys acted normal. Alex just wondered if they really would finish that table.

She wasn't too worried about Adam anymore—at least not about his broken heart, anyway. If Alyssa had dumped him, he seemed to be over it. He was laughing and having fun with Jenna and his other friends. He didn't even seem to be bothered when Alyssa/Trevor and Natalie/Simon hung out together in front of him. Alex just thought it was weird that they would parade around considering what had supposedly happened.

Δ Δ Δ

At lunch, Alex heard Jessie and Jenna gossiping about it.

"Your brother really did get shafted, didn't he?" Jessie said in her usual to-the-point way.

"I wouldn't say *shafted*," Jenna answered. "There's probably more to the story than we realize."

Jenna did not like that Adam was starting to flirt

with girls—in fact, she made that gesture with her mouth and her finger where she gagged herself any time the subject came up. But she also didn't like anyone other than herself even remotely putting him down.

"It's just too weird," Jenna said, turning to Alex. "Why does everyone act crazy about boys? And about my brother? Ewww!"

Alex put her granola down; she was done. She didn't think Adam liked her as anything more than a friend. But if he did, as Valerie said, that would completely have freaked her out, and Jenna, too. *Ugh, this is so not me!* Alex thought.

"I definitely do not want to talk about boys," she added.

▲ ▲ ▲

Later, Alex and Val headed to free swim as usual. They had become regular partners by default ever since their respective "friend breakups." Alex kept hoping that Brynn would just come up to her and apologize or at least try to work it out. They couldn't go home for the summer not speaking. That would be awful. But instead of the two of them making up, things just kept getting worse.

Brynn was walking to the shoreline holding hands with Sarah and laughing so loud that people in Los Angeles could probably have heard her. Even though Alex and Val were only a few feet away, Brynn didn't even bother to acknowledge their presence.

At least Sarah and Val were being civil to each other even if they weren't best friends anymore. Brynn was just being impossible. Alex didn't understand what was going on, or what she had done.

"I'm going to talk to her," Alex said to Valerie after they jumped off. The girls were dripping wet, and they were tired from playing Frisbee earlier. Brynn was sitting with Natalie on the blanket, and Alex thought that would be as good a time as ever to work their differences out.

"Are you sure? You want me to go with you?" Valerie said, looking at her waterproof watch. If Alex was going to talk to Brynn, she didn't have much time. Free period was over in five minutes, and then they had to hurry to their Color War meeting to find out which teams they were on.

"I'll be fine, but thanks," Alex said, feeling scared about speaking to Brynn. But she also just wanted to get it over with. This not talking for a few days was just ridiculous. They'd barely gone an hour without speaking before!

Alex headed toward the girls, forcing herself to stop thinking about how mad she was and focus on smoothing it out. Val had been telling her in woodworking not to think any bad thoughts—about herself or about Brynn. Val insisted that not dwelling on drama kind of made it undramatic (and that was a good thing!). Alex thought about how she and Val were kicking tail on the chess set (so what if it was because Jeremy had been helping them?). Things were going slightly better for Alex, so she hoped that Brynn would come around, too.

Natalie and Alyssa watched wide-eyed as Alex walked toward the three of them. They started gathering their notebooks and lotion, taking the hint to go somewhere else.

"Thanks, you two," Alex told them. Then she looked Brynn in the eyes. "Can we talk, Brynn?" she asked. Alex kept standing while Brynn changed positions on her blanket. Alex felt like a tree that was getting ready to topple over.

"I have nothing to say to you, Alex Kim," Brynn answered, not even looking up from her teen magazine.

"Come on, we've been best friends for so long. We can talk about this," Alex said, thinking about how she kind of missed whispering to Brynn before they fell asleep at night. She missed their inside jokes, and she missed jumping rope together. They had been practicing the double ropes all summer because Brynn complained that she wasn't coordinated enough.

Brynn said jumping rope made her feel more athletic. Alex had a blast teaching it to her. When they had done it, with Jenna and Valerie taking turns twirling the ropes, Alex remembered feeling how great it was to just hang out and get along. It was like they all had a rhythm that went together.

Where has our friendship gone? Alex wondered, lost in her daydream.

"What are you just standing there for?" Brynn asked, annoyed and flipping the pages of the magazine so hard, they almost ripped. "We're not best friends anymore. Can't you just deal with that?"

Ouch, Alex thought. *That was low.* She had meant well, but she didn't know what to say to Brynn anymore.

"Just go hang out with your new best friend, Valerie," Brynn said, not caring that Chelsea and Karen were just a few feet away. Chelsea wasn't even trying to act like she wasn't listening.

Alex was still standing there, and she was still about to topple over. She had to will away her tears. They were going to fall down her face and embarrass her if she didn't run away soon.

But before she took off, she added, "Fine. Then you go have fun with *your* new best friend, Sarah."

Alex stomped away, heading toward the bunk as quickly as her legs would take her.

▲ ▲ ▲

Back at the bunk, Alex couldn't hold back any longer. She was crying. Really crying. Alex wondered if Adam had felt a little bit like this—totally heartbroken—when Alyssa had dumped him. Alex thought that losing your best friend had to be about a million times worse.

Everyone at free swim had seen the whole thing, even if they hadn't heard what the girls had said. But Valerie was the only girl who followed Alex back to 3C. She hugged Alex and asked her what happened. Alex explained, thankful that she had someone she could count on.

Valerie was turning out to be a much better friend than Brynn had been lately. Maybe they really would be best friends one day—but that couldn't happen overnight. Camp was almost ending, and Alex didn't know for sure if Valerie would be back next summer. Alex would be—she always came back.

"I have an idea that might make you feel better," Valerie said, rubbing Alex's back and handing her tissues. "Do you really miss Brynn?"

"You know, even though she's been impossible lately, I do miss the old Brynn," Alex said, definitely not missing the new Brynn. "We had so much fun together before she started working on *Peter Pan*. I don't know what's gotten into her, really."

"Okay, then," Valerie went on, "I have an idea. . . . But it's kind of weird, and you just have to hear me out."

"Go for it," Alex said, slouching and pulling her knapsack close to her like a security blanket.

"We should do something nice for them," Valerie added, reaching up to mess with her braids as if she were nervous. "Brynn and Sarah, I mean."

"Who? Brynn? Why? She's been nothing but nasty," Alex said. She really did think she had tried as hard as she could. "The ball is in Brynn's court now."

"Don't let her make the decisions for you," Valerie said. "Why don't we make little friendship boxes in woodshop for Brynn and Sarah? Let's just put a note inside them that says, 'Whatever happens, remember the good times when we're all apart next fall. Good luck with everything.' Or something like that."

"Why on Earth would we go to all that trouble for *them*?" Alex asked. She was totally bewildered by Valerie's suggestion. But her tears were drying up at least, and that was a good thing.

"Because it's just the nice thing to do," Valerie added. "My mom gave me this idea. Whenever someone really ticks you off, and you've done all you can do, just give them a nice token of friendship, like a note or gift, and know that you've done the right thing. My mom brings my dad M&M's, his favorite kind—the peanut ones— whenever they've been at each other's throats, no matter who is right or wrong. And you know what? They always stop fighting. No one stays mad when you do something nice for them."

"I don't know about this," Alex said, getting up so

she could get dressed for the Color War meeting—she sure wasn't missing *that*.

"Let's just give it a try," Valerie said, getting up, too. "Instead of the chess set. Our friendships are more important than some game, right? We still have a few more days of woodworking. It can't hurt."

"What about the stool for your dad that you were working on?" Alex asked, thinking of ways to get out of going through with this crazy plan. It really did seem like Brynn should be making *her* something nice, but Alex tried to stay open-minded about Valerie's idea.

"I finished it. Jeremy helped me yesterday," Valerie yelled from the shower.

She didn't have anything to lose. Alex decided she'd try it. She did feel kind of good about doing something sweet, even if it was for Brynn. Valerie's suggestion made a little bit of sense, she guessed. Alex was always volunteering to help everyone—especially the counselors—because it made her happy to do so. Good deeds had a way of boosting Alex's self-confidence. And she could definitely use a boost, she figured.

At the very least, things certainly couldn't get any worse.

▲ ▲ ▲

The Color War meeting was the best. At least Alex thought so. The whole camp—hundreds of kids of all ages—arrived for the meeting after dinner. There was a small campfire burning near the flagpole. Dr. Steve stood behind the fire, creating a stage for himself, as if he were presenting the Oscar nominations or something. Every kid sat with his or her bunk, excited, knowing that the "enemy" could be sitting right beside you. Once they got their assignments, bunkmate would compete against bunkmate for the victory.

But before that happened, everyone sang silly songs like "Green and Yeller" and "Who Stole My Tree?" to get pumped up. Then Dr. Steve made everyone hold hands and meditate (Alex couldn't believe he added meditation to his weirdness this summer) as a show of solidarity before giving his speech.

Dr. Steve went on for twenty whole minutes, just like he did every year, about sportsmanship and no pranks and healthy competition and team pride and camp rivalry and even went on a tangent about how Color War could teach every person about world peace.

"The leaders of our world should come to Camp Lakeview!" he yelled, waving his fishing hat in the air. The kids only clapped a little bit—mostly, just the counselors cheered because he was, after all, their eccentric boss. Alex and Valerie couldn't help but giggle.

"Oh my dog," Valerie said, rolling her eyes and nudging Alex in the side. "He's not even kidding!"

"Oh yes, he means every word," Alex added.

Then, amid hundreds of hushed, anxious campers, the envelopes were handed out. That was something different they were doing this year. Every camper was getting a sealed letter with his or her team assignment on it. For some reason, Dr. Steve thought it would be good for each camper to try to keep his or her team assignment a secret until breakfast the next morning. Then, after breakfast, the competition lists would be posted outside of each cabin.

Color War took place over two days and consisted

of a mix of group events and division events. Group events—where kids of all ages competed together in games like singdown and potato-sack race—were worth fifty points for the winners. Division events—where kids competed for their teams against their own age group during games like Scrabble and tug-o-war—were worth twenty-five points for the winners. There were four group events, two per day of Color War, and several division events. The counselors had to do a lot of planning!

Alex couldn't get on board with the secret thing. How was she going to get to bed that night without somehow letting it slip?

"The point is to absolutely torture us, which clearly he considers to be great fun," Valerie said.

But Alex suspected another reason they were doing it this way. Last year, the Blues stayed up all night making confetti that they threw in the mess hall oatmeal. Maybe he was trying to keep night-before pranks to a minimum. Or maybe this was just another "camp challenge."

Julie handed Alex her envelope, and she tore it open. Inside, there was a blank white paper with a small blue dot in the center. Alex was thrilled to be a Blue. It was her favorite color, so it had to be lucky. She just hoped that her closest 3C friends were Blues, too.

"What'd you get?" Valerie whispered.

"What'd you get?" Candace yelled before Jessie could put her hand over Candace's mouth.

"I'm not telling till tomorrow." Alex smiled.

And just then, red and blue balloons fell from a net that was suspended between several trees. Alex was so excited—the next few days would definitely make up for the recent bad ones.

After two more rounds of "Green and Yeller," all the kids headed back to their bunks—some keeping the secret, some surely not—screaming and yelling and acting like wild safari animals.

Camp is awesome, Alex thought. *This is the whole reason I came.*

"Twinkie time!" Jenna yelled as she ripped open a cardboard box from her parents that night. Julie and Marissa were out at a staff meeting, and so it was party time in 3C. Alex dreaded party time. The other girls looked forward to sharing the treats. But sharing time was always a nightmare for Alex.

"I'll give one to anyone who reveals their team!" she yelled.

"I'm a Blue!" Chelsea yelled. Alex hoped she was just lying, but knowing her own luck lately, she probably wasn't.

"I'm a Red!" Jessie chimed in. "No wait, a Blue! No wait, a Red!"

With that, Twinkies started flying through the air. "Nice pass," Grace yelled as she caught hers.

Chelsea, Karen, Brynn, Sarah, and Valerie tore into theirs. Alex could hear the cellophane wrappers crinkle. She could hear her bunkmates chewing, *mmm-ing,* and *ahhh-ing.*

She knew as soon as Chelsea took the last bite and wiped her mouth, she'd be all over Alex as usual. But worse, Alex couldn't control herself any longer. She wanted to eat one of those Twinkies so bad that she could taste it. It had been seven months—maybe longer—since she'd had such a yummy, sweet, sugary, totally-bad-for-you treat.

"Alex?" Jenna asked, ever polite even though Alex never said yes. She—like everyone else—just assumed Alex was a health nut.

Jenna didn't get it into her head that Alex wished she would stop asking her. To Jenna, not offering a bite to everyone was bad manners. With so many siblings, it was part of her genetic makeup to share. Jenna didn't understand that she was actually torturing Alex.

"I, um," Alex started to say. All eyes were, once again, on her. She hadn't eaten the Nerds or the more recent chocolate peanut butter cookies. And Chelsea had been all over her both times.

In fact, just yesterday, Karen—*Karen of all mousy people!*—had taken Alex aside and asked her if everything was all right. "I, um, like, saw you looking kind of greenish-yellow at free swim the other day," Karen had said one night before bed. "You know, right when you and Brynn started having that fight. You can, um, like, tell me if something's wrong," Karen had added.

Alex appreciated the concern, but she was losing her patience. She told Karen she was fine and offered to look at her sticker collection—just to change the subject. Alex was going to shred the entire camp's pillows. That's how tired she was of everything that had been going on lately. She was sick of Chelsea's nasty words about "Little Miss Perfect" having to stay in shape for soccer.

Alex's walls were coming down.

"You know what? Throw me one," Alex said to Jenna.

"Really? Cool!" Jenna said, glad to oblige. She tossed the Twinkie across the room to her friend.

Alex caught it easily. She didn't squish or harm the Twinkie. *Who knew athletic ability would help keep your snacks safe?* Alex thought. The other girls clapped and whooped. And Alex loved being cheered on, whatever the reason. It just felt good. It felt like belonging. And Alex had been feeling so left out for so long now.

She scarfed that Twinkie down in three seconds flat.

"*Mmm*," she said loudly. "That was good!"

"You want another one?" Jenna asked.

"I do!" Brynn yelled.

"Me first!" Grace begged.

"Really, I only have one more, girls," Jenna said. "Alex has missed out on all the other snacks. If she wants it, it should be hers."

"I'll take it," Alex said. She opened the other one, wide-eyed. She took one small bite, and then she got up to tuck it into a plastic box in her cubbyhole.

"That *so* won't be there tomorrow," Chelsea said. "I'm going to eat it."

"You will not, or I'll kick your butt," Valerie said.

The girls laughed and enjoyed their short-lived sugar high. They had almost calmed down by the time Julie and Marissa returned from their meeting.

It took at least two more hours before the girls stopped whispering and gossiping in the dark. There was no way anyone was going to get a good night's sleep that night—not with Color War starting tomorrow. Even though Alex had been having a really difficult couple of days, just for that evening, she could forget about it all. She pretended that she was just like everyone else, like she fit in. Sharing in their snacks and pillow fights was freeing. She didn't have to pretend she was writing a letter or reading a book so they would leave her alone. She just jumped right in to join the fun—Twinkies and all. She was determined not to let anything, not even sweet treats— freak her out.

chapter
SEVEN

The real roar of wild animals erupted early the next morning.

Bunk 3C was totally not surprised.

It was the first day of Color War, after all.

Instead of Julie's friendly, chirpy morning call of, "Wakey, Wakey!" the girls heard kids outside yelling things like, "Be prepared to get eaten alive!" and "Wake up and get ready to go dowwwwnnn!" and "Red will rule the entire free world!" A whole bunch of kids were up an hour early and running through the bunks in celebration.

No one was supposed to tell a soul which team they were on until the kick-off breakfast that morning, but some kids clearly broke the rule as soon as last night's meeting was adjourned. This year's Reds—at least the ones with hyena giggles and lion roars—obviously weren't concerned about the rules at that moment. They made so much noise—some of them even had lifeguard whistles to blow and pots and pans to clang—that sleeping was no longer an option for anyone.

The crazy Red strategy was obvious. Many

of them had gotten themselves to sleep early the night before—those who'd revealed themselves, that is—rose earlier, and then woke up the rest of the camp up. They clearly wanted the Blue team to be tired for the first day of competition. It was a sneaky, sneaky move. Alex admired their ability to work together and strategize, but she also thought the Reds were being silly. Surely, some of their team members would be tired, too. Especially the Reds who were in her bunk still chatting away about boys, life, camp, and one another until the late, late hours of last night.

At least I feel really good this morning, Alex thought. She had been worried that the night before would have her worn out, maybe even sick, for the all-important competitions. But she was fine.

Woohoo! This is great, she couldn't help thinking.

She looked around the bunk, and several girls were missing. The 3C Reds had sneaked out to participate in the morning mayhem. *Now that was really impressive,* Alex thought. She couldn't believe she had been sleeping so soundly that she hadn't heard them earlier. She looked around, seeing who was there and who was not. Her heart sunk. She had wanted certain people to be on her team, and those certain people's beds were empty.

After the initial shock of hearing the noise and seeing who was (and wasn't) on her team, Alex decided there was nothing else to do but make the best of it. She'd have to pump herself up.

There is nothing I love more than Color War, she told herself. She remembered the two whole days of outdoor activities—an all-out Alex fest around Camp Lakeview. Sure, she was surprised that she had liked woodworking as much as she had. But no matter how great it had been to finish a cutting board and to start on the chess set, it was still more fun to punt a soccer ball. Alex's first love was sports, especially soccer. It was time to play ball!

△ △ △

Breakfast was mayhem. As usual, on the start of Color War, excitement hung in the air. Kids were yelling, others were telling tall tales about their athletic abilities, others still were hurling muffins and burned toast through the air. She tried to get down some food before kids started spraying silly string—a harmless Color War ritual aimed at ruining the opposite team's morning meal.

A stripe of electric blue shot through the air and landed on her empty plate, narrowly avoiding her cup of water. She wiped her mouth and licked her lips. She smiled. The silly string had missed her watery eggs. She'd already downed everything—somehow—and she was already feeling lucky about the day to follow. Her fingers were crossed.

"Red! Red! Red! We are the best!" someone yelled. Alex heard, and her stomach dropped just like it had earlier that morning in the bunk. It was the voice of someone who'd been absent from the bunk that morning.

It was, unmistakably, Brynn's voice.

When Alex looked up, Brynn was in the front of the long, narrow room doing a cheer with Sarah and a few other girls right in the middle of the mess hall. All eyes were on Brynn, and people were laughing, screaming, or booing—or all three together.

Alex didn't mind the confetti or the cheerleading act. What Alex really minded was that she was a Blue and that Brynn was a Red. In all the years they'd come to camp together, they'd always been on the same team. Sarah was, as fate would have it, a Red, too.

Alex couldn't help but be jealous that Brynn and Sarah would get to spend *more* time together—bonding, laughing, and strategizing. Alex was pitted against her friends—or ex-friends, as the case was—and she was totally uncomfortable with it. She knew she was a strong athlete and Scrabble player, so that wasn't the issue. Alex could compete with anyone at camp. It was just that Alex usually coached Brynn and Sarah and cheered *them* on. The one thing that worried Alex was how skilled Brynn could be at mind games, which was another important element of competition.

Alex knew she could beat Brynn physically, but she wasn't so sure how she'd do against her in the more creative stuff like singdown. Overall, Alex was just sad that they wouldn't be together this year.

"Okay, kids!" Dr. Steve yelled on the mess hall PA system. "We're posting the official team lists outside of the mess hall. You can share your team assignments now!"

"Why the long face, Sport?" a high voice screeched behind her. It was Jenna's, and Grace stood at her side. "We're all Blues! Can you believe it?!"

At least *something* good had happened. Jenna and Alex had never been on the same Color War team. They figured they had been separated on purpose. Really, it was more fair that way, since they were both really good at sports. But this year, who knew what could happen?

The Color War isn't looking so bad after all, Alex told herself.

"We've got to make some signs at the Blue pep rally

and put the brakes on those Reds," Jenna said, already wearing a blue T-shirt and shorts, looking ready for a game.

"I'm a better cheerleader than those chicks, anyway," Grace said, joking. That was probably true, too. Grace was always happy and smiling, and she would be a great member of Alex's team. She really would be good at keeping everyone's spirit up. Maybe Alex didn't need Brynn, after all.

"Don't worry, Alex," Grace said, totally reading her friend's mind. "Everything will be okay," she added. It was nice to know that other people could see what was going on, even if Alex couldn't talk about it. Alex refused to think like that for another second. She willed herself to snap out of her funk. Color War was her favorite time—it was a time to shine and show the Red Team what tough stuff she was made of. She just hoped Valerie was on her team.

She thought to herself, *I know I can, I know I can.*

"We're so going to get them," Jenna said. "Even if Chelsea is on our team."

"She is?!!!" Alex said, not even being careful to hide her feelings for the nasty blonde. "I'd hoped she was lying last night."

"I know—ugh," Jenna said. She made a face.

"Come on, let's not think about that right now," Grace added. "I'll work on getting the blond beast in a good mood, and I'll try to get her to play on the Scrabble team." Chelsea was good at word games. The girls hoped that she would turn out to be a useful member of the Blues, and not a total storm cloud.

"Oh, I don't want to think about her. Let's go to

our Blue rally. Let's make some killer signs," Jenna said. "I've been stashing art supplies all summer for this very occasion. I just need you all to come up with ideas."

"So, is Valerie on our team, too?" Jenna asked.

"Yeah, that's what she told me," Grace said. "You, me, Chelsea, Natalie, Alyssa, Alex, and Valerie."

That left Karen, Candace, Brynn, Sarah, and Jessie on Red. *It was weird for the teams to be uneven*, Alex thought. There must have been an uneven number somewhere else in the division that they were compensating for.

Jenna and Alex shared a knowing glance, and Jenna said, "Grace, go grab Valerie some toast and bagels. The Reds will steal all the food soon. People don't compete as well when they're hungry. Alex, do you need some snacks, too?"

"No, I'm good," Alex answered.

"What about you, Grace?" Jenna asked.

"I'm all filled up and ready to *par-tay*," she said, putting some treats in her pockets for Valerie and whoever else didn't get a chance to eat. She was fighting kids from the Red Team who were up there hoarding stuff, too.

Why does food always have to be such a big deal? Alex wondered as she ran over to the arts and crafts shack for the Blue rally.

The crackle of the PA system indicated a new announcement from Dr. Steve.

"Apparently," he said, clearing his throat, "from the outburst this morning, we saw that one team in particular—some members of the Reds, specifically—didn't keep their team affiliation secret. As a result, all Reds will get a twenty-five point deduction!"

Some Reds hissed and booed and threw bagels at

the Reds who had set up the abrupt morning wake-up.

"So, Blues, you have an advantage. Use it wisely. Now good luck to you all!"

The Blues—Alex, Jenna, Grace, Val, Alyssa, Natalie, and even Chelsea—whooped and screamed in celebration.

▲ ▲ ▲

Day One started with a rally. Marissa had made everyone blue wristbands, and Jenna and Alex made some kick-tail signs. They sung songs like "We Are the Champions" as they got ready for the big competition. Both days would start with a camp-wide competition— today's was the singdown. Then the divisions broke up and, instead of their regular free-choice activities, there were division competitions.

The first one each day would be sports, like basketball or soccer, and the second one after lunch would be a less athletic, like blob tag (*so funny*, Alex thought) and Scrabble. This went on for two days, and full schedules were posted on each bunk. In the evenings, kids could work on their missed activities (*like woodworking*, Alex realized) if they wanted to during free time.

Since much of Color War dealt with athletic ability, endurance, and prowess, Jenna and Alex went back to the bunk with the others to put their heads together to strategize for their division soccer game. As long as they let Julie know where they'd be, they were allowed a little more independence during "Color War–designated hours." When the competition ended for the day—or during meals, of course—everyone traveled as a bunk again.

As they scribbled "We're seeing BLUE!" and "BLUE will rock your world" on pieces of poster board, they plotted out ways to win.

▲ ▲ ▲

Since Scrabble would be soon, Alex knew the time had come for her heart-to-heart with Chelsea. Chelsea was really good at the game, so she could help the Blues earn their twenty-five points. And the only goal for Alex was to win, win, win.

Alex tracked her down in the bunk and willed herself to be patient with her grumpy teammate.

Needless to say, Chelsea did not exactly appreciate the pep talk. "Whatever. I know what this is about. You just won't be able to stand it if I'm better than you, right?" she said, wrinkling her nose.

Alex, for the first time, actually felt sorry for Chelsea. When she stopped and thought about it, Chelsea rarely smiled. Even when she got to do something she liked—like Scrabble—she didn't seem to enjoy it.

She just seems like she doesn't know how to be happy, Alex thought. Again, for the first time, Alex didn't get mad at Chelsea. Instead, she pitied her. She thought Chelsea's entire existence was just sad.

"I need you to be the best, Chelsea, even if that's better than me," Alex said. "I don't care which one of us wins, as long as *we* win together. It's all about the Blues. It's not about me. And it's not about you, either."

Chelsea just stuck out her tongue and answered, "Always Little Miss Perfect . . . *always*." With that, she pranced away to talk to Karen.

Meanwhile, on the other side of the bunk, right in

Alex's line of vision, she could see Brynn hugging Sarah—overdramatically. Brynn glanced at Alex just to make sure that, yes, Alex had seen the two of them bonding—*without* Alex. Alex smiled at Brynn. Alex didn't want Brynn to think she was getting to her, even if Brynn kind of was. To Alex, Color War was healthy competition; maybe it was a healthier way to work through their differences.

Heck, she'd tried everything else, hadn't she?

▲ ▲ ▲

Alex, Jenna, and Val headed out to the porch to work on a Blue Team cheer. Jenna was frantically racking her brain for a word that rhymed with "stupendous" when Alex heard a familiar voice.

"Too bad we're on different teams, Alex."

Alex looked up. Adam was making his way toward the bunk. She thought he was actually on his way somewhere else, but then he stopped and stood there like he wanted to talk. Alex was happy to see him, but she was also nervous. Something was up, definitely. She noticed the way he was sweating, too. Then he added, "So are you and Valerie both Blue?"

Something in Alex's brain clicked. Maybe Adam Spasm had been hanging around all of the time because of Valerie. *He likes her!* Alex thought. That made sense to Alex—Valerie was confident, cool, outgoing, cute.

Adam and Val? Alex thought as she noticed an ant crawling across her sneaker.

"And Jenna, too," Alex said, her heart beating a little too hard. "We're going to *kill* the Reds."

Her *words* were confident. So why was her body shaking like the laundry spin cycle?

I do not want to think about crushes and stuff, she thought. *Especially not now. I need to focus.*

"*Maybe* you girls will survive without me," Adam joked, "but don't be so sure."

"Yeah, *maybe!*" Valerie called after him, shaking a fist menacingly.

"He's *so* weird," she said, once he had gone.

"Yeah, what was that!?" Jenna asked, being nosy.

"Right?" Alex asked. Her heart rate had returned to normal and the flush she'd felt in her cheeks had cooled. And Jenna seemed clueless that Alex had even been thinking . . .

Nothing! You were thinking nothing!

"Let's get back to that cheer," Val said, nudging them both. The small smile on her face suggested that *she* might have an idea what Alex was thinking.

Nothing, Alex reminded herself firmly. *Nothing at all.*

▲ ▲ ▲

"And fifty points goes to the Blues for the singdown!" Pete yelled. He smiled. His face was painted red, and he wore a headband with devil horns to show his spirit. Even though his team hadn't won the first competition, he was just as enthusiastic and happy for the Blues. He was a great sport.

Marissa, a Blue, turned to her team. "You guys rock."

"When you came up with song that had the word 'burger' in it, I was so impressed!" Marissa said to Alyssa.

"Cheeseburger in Paradise? A classic," Nat quipped, clapping her friend on the back good-naturedly.

Alyssa only grinned, semi-embarrassed at her retro-music knowledge.

Alex, Jenna, Grace, Valerie, Natalie, Alyssa, and Chelsea had another competition together that day. They were on the same tug-o-war team. Alex knew that she'd be against Brynn and Sarah there. Brynn loved that game, and she had a will as strong as chain links.

"Don't worry about them," Valerie said as the teams lined up on either side of the thick, white rope. Val reminded Alex that they had to finish their wooden boxes—their gifts to their ex-friends—later that night during their evening free time. Working on a gift for Brynn was just about the last thing Alex wanted to do. "Whether you two are close friends again or not," Valerie explained, "with these gifts, at least you two won't be enemies."

"We'll be frenemies, instead," Alex said, wondering how she'd let Valerie talk her into this crazy gift idea.

"Are you talking about Brynn?" Chelsea said, interrupting.

Alex and Valerie immediately clammed up. They definitely didn't want Chelsea to get involved. Chelsea would surely think of a backhanded putdown or something—anything—wicked to say.

"Please. Like I don't know what's going on," Chelsea snorted.

"Nothing's going on," Alex insisted, looking across the thick competition rope for Brynn. Brynn was laughing—make that cackling—about something with Sarah.

Instead of getting sad, Alex got determined. The girls lined up for tug-o-war, bracing their legs and feet into the ground as if they could grow roots.

"On your mark, get set, go!" Julie yelled. She was the counselor-in-charge once again. She had on an all-red outfit, and had painted cat whiskers on her face. Alex didn't know what that had to do with anything, but it was funny.

"One, two, three!" Jenna yelled, telling them to all yank together. She was the anchor of the team, meaning she stood at the end of the rope, her feet and body leaning toward the earth. Jenna was the strongest of the group, so she was the unofficial team leader for that game.

The immediate strain on the rope knocked the wind out of Alex and dragged her off her feet, taking her completely by surprise. Her strength was draining away, as if the rope was actually sucking it out of her body.

Shake it off, she thought, determined to keep trying. Her grip was so tight that it burned. She looked up and saw Brynn's eyes shut, her face scrunched up into a wrinkled ball. Brynn loved tug-o-war, and it looked like she was about to win at it. Unbelievably, Alex's confidence sagged.

Slowly, the Red Team inched their way backward. The Blues' bottoms hit the ground as their last bit of sheer willpower washed away. They slid forward, defeated.

"Go, Red!" Julie yelled. "We rule!"

Brynn and Sarah and Candace and Jessie and Karen hugged one another. Tears nearly sprung from Alex's eyes. She couldn't believe the Blues had lost. She blamed herself because she hadn't tried hard enough. She couldn't believe that she was an outsider to her ex-best friend.

"It's okay," Jenna said. "None of them are good at

basketball. They might as well take this win while they can get one."

"Except for Sarah, she's, like, good at everything," Chelsea said in a voice that was much more quiet than usual.

Chelsea was right—Sarah was a great athlete. But Alex team-hugged Jenna. Together, they wouldn't let the Reds win again.

I think I can, I think I can, Alex thought to herself.

I have to.

Alex started strategizing. She wondered and calculated and figured what she'd have to do to get back in the right mindset to win. She thought of the Ninja Supertwins. In tug-o-war, she had her former best friend's determination and spirit. It was what she loved best about Brynn, and seeing it had made her wistful. That sad, longing feeling took away Alex's competitive edge. Alex was uncomfortable playing against Brynn; it was like an allergic reaction. It made her throat get thick and her head ache. Alex turned her thoughts to soccer that afternoon. It would be easier.

▲ ▲ ▲

After lunch, the bunk headed off to the soccer field. Alex rubbed her temples. Her head thumped with a dull thud. As her mind wandered, Alex realized that she'd left her knapsack in the bunk. She figured she was just tired from the night before. *I'm fine,* she told herself. Then her head started to spin. She paused, glancing back toward the bunk.

"I, um, just have to grab one thing. I'll be back in five minutes," Alex said.

"Oh, no you don't," Natalie said, smiling and teasing Alex. "I know you don't really want to compete against Brynn again. I could see it during tug-o-war. But you're not bailing on us for soccer. We *need* you for soccer."

"I'll be right back, I just have to go—" Alex started to say.

"Let's go, girls! We're running late!" Julie yelled. "Everyone on the soccer field! It's time for midfield shots."

"Midfield shots!" Candace yelled, crazy enthusiastic even though she wasn't so good at them.

Jenna cheered. Nat shrugged and winked at Alyssa. Grace and Valerie clapped like crazy because they were awesome cheerleaders.

Alex watched as Brynn and Sarah started frowning. Clearly, those two knew that the next round would be tougher for them than tug-o-war had been. Alex told herself to get excited and to do it fast. Soccer was her *thing*.

"Alex, you okay?" Julie asked, breaking into Alex's thoughts.

"I'm fine," Alex answered, even though her brain was throbbing as if a jackhammer was right next to her head.

"You sure? You seem tired," Julie added.

Before Julie could make a big deal out of anything, Alex turned toward her teammates.

"Okay, girls. I've got an idea. Here's how we're going to win," Alex said, drawing the Blue team into a huddle.

After, the girls, Blue and Red, lined up on opposite

sides of the goal net. They would take turns kicking three-point shots, kind of like a game of H-O-R-S-E, but using a soccer ball and with points. Everyone had three turns. If you hit either edge of the net, you got one point. Hitting the edge of the goal got your team two points. Scoring a goal was three full points. At the end of the game, the points were dropped, but the winning team added a full twenty-five to their team's overall total.

Alex forgot that she needed her knapsack and willed her headache to calm down so she could concentrate. It didn't matter if Brynn was prancing around with Sarah. It didn't matter if they were on opposite teams. It didn't matter if she was still getting over Brynn's decision to be mad at her. Alex still loved being the athlete. She figured she deserved to shine in her element.

She deserved to win.

"You can do it, Brynn," Sarah yelled as her friend stood poised to kick.

Alex didn't get down this time like she had during tug-o-war. She stood there, watching what Brynn would do with the ball, and she thought of the day as a competition, not as anything to do with the breakup of their years of friendship.

Brynn tried to look focused, but she kept glancing over at Alex. Alex was glassy-eyed, staring at Brynn's kicks instead of looking directly at Brynn. Brynn missed all of them.

Alex was up next. Valerie and Jenna patted her back and told Alex how awesome she was before she made her way to the line. Alex dribbled the ball nine times before going for her first kick.

Sure!

Her team cheered because she'd made a goal, scoring three whole points. Alex's heart pounded. She was so intent on scoring nine points that she didn't pay attention to anything else. Her energy had drained. Her breath was short. Her heart fluttered.

She thought she was just pumped to win.

She dribbled ten more times, slowly, her eyes never leaving the net. She lifted her right foot to launch the ball into the perfect position in the air. On one side, her team members stood in anxious silence—giving Alex the moral support she needed to concentrate. On the other side, the girls screamed and yelled, trying to break her thoughts and her lucky streak.

Alex felt like she was in a movie. She could see both teams of girls moving in slow motion, the outlines of their faces and bodies going grainy, like a blurry photograph.

Alex didn't think anything of how fuzzy she was getting. She thought it was just the buzz of adrenaline. She didn't realize what was happening.

She didn't realize she was going down.

Hard.

chapter EIGHT

"Oh my God!" Brynn yelled.

Alex could barely make out her former friend's voice through her haze. Through tiny slits in her mostly closed eyes, she saw Brynn's face hovering anxiously overhead.

The rest of the girls were stiff with worry. Valerie looked on the verge of tears. Jenna ran off, yelling to the others that she was going to the infirmary to get the nurse. Sarah stood back, uncertain. In a surprise move, Chelsea hovered nervously at Alex's side.

"Where's your knapsack?!" Julie asked, about to hyperventilate herself. "We need your knapsack."

"She left it in the bunk," Valerie yelled, pulling herself together.

"I know where it is, I'll get it," Chelsea said, running off before anyone else could do it.

Julie patted Alex's face gently, trying to keep her awake.

"Alex, honey, come on. Don't pass out. Stay awake. We're here, and we're going to take care of you. Help us out by staying awake, honey," Julie said.

Julie was trying to stay calm, but it was clear that

she was worried. Her hands were shaking uncontrollably. "Come on. You can do it.

"Jenna went to the infirmary, right?" Julie asked, turning to the rest of the group.

"Yeah, what can we do? Just tell us what to do!" Valerie asked, pacing around Alex.

"What's wrong with her, Julie?" Brynn asked, desperation in her voice. "What's wrong?"

Brynn's face was turning blotchy red. Brynn was much more upset than anyone else—and she wasn't even being overdramatic for once.

Sweaty and breathless, Chelsea appeared back on the scene, Alex's navy blue backpack in her hands. Julie grabbed it, and she fished around frantically inside. She pulled out the little tablets that Valerie had seen earlier and also a small bottle of water.

"Alex," Julie said, breathing fast and quick. "Keep your eyes open, just keep them open for me. I'll take care of you. We'll take care of you."

"What? What happened?" Alex murmured softly as she kinda-sorta began to wake up.

"Oh thank God," Julie said, her voice quivering. Sweat drops lined the sides of Julie's face. "Open your mouth."

"Look under my bed," Alex mumbled to Brynn, who was sitting on the ground just to Alex's left side. Alex's eyelids fluttered as if she were having a super difficult time keeping them open. "My kit's there."

Brynn wiped the tears from her eyes. Her shoulders were slumped—so unlike her usual confident stance—as she ran off toward the bunk in a blur.

Julie pried open Alex's mouth and placed an

unwrapped candy between Alex's lips. Then Julie poured water, also from Alex's knapsack, over the candy and into Alex's mouth. A whole lot of the liquid ran down the sides of Alex's face. But her eyes began to stay open, and her eyelids stopped fluttering so much.

Just seconds later, the nurse arrived with an oxygen tank and a couple of counselors. Brynn was not back yet.

"Good job, Julie, good job," the nurse said. "I'm really impressed. Now, girls, please step back." The nurse whispered something gently to Alex. The counselors whisked Alex away to the infirmary. She was mumbling to them, "Did we win? Did we win?"

The rest of the girls rushed to Julie, and Julie struggled to catch her breath. Her forehead was sweating, and she leaned over her knees, trying to get herself together. Brynn arrived on the scene with a little white medicine box, totally out of breath.

"I don't think I've ever been so scared in my life," Julie said, more to herself than to the girls. "That was close."

"What's wrong with her?! What's wrong with Alex?!" Brynn yelled, upset.

"The nurse has her, Brynn," Julie said, patting her back. "And now she has her kit, too. She's going to be okay now."

"Are you sure?" Valerie asked. She paced around the group of girls, rubbing the palms of her hands together.

"She has juvenile diabetes," Chelsea said, interrupting. She sat down on the ground and rubbed her temples.

"How did *you* know?" Julie asked surprised. "She didn't tell anyone."

"My cousin has it," Chelsea said. "It's awful. Really awful."

"So you knew about Alex this whole time, and you still always give her a hard time about eating snacks?" Valerie asked, clearly annoyed.

"I didn't know!" Chelsea said, still not making eye contact with anyone. "I just figured it out when I saw the tablets Julie put in Alex's mouth. I swear! I didn't know until a second ago!" With that, she stood up and ran back to the bunk.

"An insulin kit, thank you, dear," Nurse Helen said, taking Alex's box from Brynn and placing it on an empty cot.

Brynn had raced Alex's kit to the infirmary. Now she stood awkwardly next to Alex's bed.

"Luckily, I also have this stuff on hand here. So do me a favor, and make sure you put this back exactly where you found it. And Alex, no more Twinkies for you, okay?"

"Okay," Alex muttered softly. Her voice was tired. She hadn't regained her normal strength yet, but at least she wasn't dizzy anymore.

"Hi," she said weakly, turning to Brynn.

"Hey, girl," Brynn said, reaching for Alex's hand.

Alex let her take it—she was in no position to do anything else. Alex's heart beat hard. She really didn't know what to say to Brynn. She did know that somehow, she was relieved to see Brynn there at the infirmary. Deep down, Alex knew that Brynn would get over whatever was eating her brain lately. Alex knew that Brynn would come through for her if she really needed her to. And Alex needed her to right then.

"Is it too late to say I'm sorry?" Brynn asked, rubbing Alex's thumb the way Alex's mother might have done if she were there.

"For what?" Alex asked, winking at Brynn.

"I've been so awful," Brynn said, her eyes tearing up for about the fifth time in the last thirty minutes. "I love you. You really had me worried just now! I couldn't bear to think that I had been so mean to you—while you were so sick!"

"I'm not that sick," Alex said. Slowly, the energy was flowing back into her veins. Her body was acting like she'd been at a slumber party all night—and hadn't slept a wink. But other than that, Alex felt okay. It definitely helped that Brynn was there—and ready to reconcile.

"You have diabetes, though!"

"I do?" Alex asked, feigning shock.

"I'm so serious! I'm not making a joke. You looked like you could've died," Brynn said, moving her head around as if she were on stage.

"Oh, I just shouldn't have eaten all that junk last night," Alex said, waving her hand as if to say *pppshaw!* "And I didn't get a shot this morning like I usually do."

"So that's where you go every day before we clean the cabin!" Brynn said, her hands in the air.

"Yes, and you thought I was staying after breakfast to help Pete," Alex answered, smirking. "That's what everyone thought, or so I hoped. Even if it meant getting teased by Chelsea."

"It all makes so much sense now," Brynn said, rubbing her forehead. "But why didn't you just tell me? When did this happen? Last year you ate all kinds of junk!"

"I got diagnosed last fall. I was tired and thirsty all the time," Alex said, a serious expression on her face. "The doctor said I'd have to totally change my diet and get shots once a day, so that's what I've been doing."

"I'm so embarrassed that you didn't think you could tell me. When you stopped eating snacks even I thought—"

"Eating disorder," Alex said, lying in the cot and turning her gaze to look out the window. "Or some weird soccer diet. I know."

"I can't believe you! Why didn't you just tell us?" Brynn asked, her voice louder. "The bunk, I mean. We would've understood. I definitely would've understood."

"First of all, everyone at school back home knows about it, and it's like I get all this attention that I don't want," Alex said, sitting up on the cot as her energy returned more and more.

She continued, "I don't want anyone to feel sorry for me, and I don't want to be known as the girl with diabetes like I am at home.

"It's so much better here. I mean, I'm just known for being good at soccer. What could be better than that?"

"Oh my God, Alex!" Brynn said, turning her voice down as the nurse looked her way. "You don't have to be perfect all the time. We would've understood—and we would've still thought you were our resident Mia Hamm. I don't get it."

"But I really don't want to cause any trouble or extra fuss. I just want things to go smoothly—and if everyone knew, I thought it would be a big deal or something,"

Alex explained, surprised at how relieved she was that she didn't have to hide it anymore. She was just sorry her bunkmates found out the way they did. Especially sorry since she passed out—she had a bruise on her butt where she smacked down onto the soccer field.

"I know I haven't been the best example of this lately," Brynn said, "but your friends accept you for who you are. If you have an issue—hello, I have about a hundred—that just makes you more interesting. I'm so sorry I was so jealous and awful to you the past few days. I thought you were choosing Valerie and Julie and your woodshop friends over me. I was just worried that you were about to dump me, and I shouldn't have acted the way I did."

"Brynn, I would never do that to you!" Alex said. "I just wanted to do my own thing—like hang out with Julie sometimes and play more soccer. But all my free time was supposed to be with you."

"I know, I know. I wasn't very nice at all. Are you going to hate me forever? Because I'm pretty sure that I would hate me forever if I were in your shoes. I mean, when I saw you passed out just now—like you were going to die or something—I have never felt so guilty and evil and awful in my whole life. I'll never act like that again. Not to anyone. Ever."

"Stop it, I'm so serious," Alex said, blushing.

Her heart was beating a lot now, but because she was happy. She could tell by the concern in Brynn's eyes that she had gotten her old best friend back. Alex couldn't have been more thrilled. At least something good had come out of her diabetic breakdown.

Alex wouldn't let herself get that bad again—she

just had to be better at watching what she ate! She would definitely stay away from the sugary treats. Julie and the others always had Alex in the kitchen to make sure there were enough diabetes-friendly goodies for her. Alex would stick to those foods—special puddings and cookies and candies made with artificial sweeteners—from now on.

Valerie and Sarah burst through the door, not even giving Helen a chance to stop them.

"Are you okay?" they asked in unison. They were panting, so it was difficult to understand what else they were trying to say.

"She's fine," Brynn said, explaining the insulin kit and Alex's drop in blood sugar that caused her to pass out and everything else she had just learned at the infirmary.

"She'll be fine, as long as you girls don't encourage her to eat sweets—*no more Twinkies*," Nurse Helen interrupted. "She can even leave now if she wants to."

"Really?!!!" Alex sprang out of her cot, and she tied her sneakers. She was ready to go canoeing.

"Take it easy today—no more sports in Color War, Alex," the nurse said. "And I want you to stop in before bed tonight."

"You've got to be kidding me!" Alex felt her heart sink. What was the point of Color War if she couldn't play sports?

"I have a feeling you'd make a great coach tomorrow," Nurse Helen said. "You have to do it. You have to give you body time to recover. You just went into diabetic shock, Alex Kim. You're lucky you're not in the hospital."

"Ahh man, that's not good," Brynn whispered into Alex's ear.

"Ugh, I know, I know," she answered, knowing

she'd just have to deal. The soccer episode had scared her to death. And she didn't want to go through that again. She'd do what she could to help the Blues from the sidelines. At least she could still play Scrabble.

One good thing: Alex had always been stopping by the infirmary to get her blood sugar levels checked—and to get her daily shot. She was tired of sneaking around and super relieved that she wouldn't have to do it ever again. The four girls joined hands and headed back to 3C.

Together.

Alex passing out on the soccer field had made everyone want to get along. All the girls were so scared—a few of them worried that Alex was really and truly dead for a moment—that everyone wanted to reaffirm their friendships. It became clear that things could change for the worse in an instant. And in the midst of that change, the girls realized that they wanted to be nicer. After all, there were only three more days left of camp.

Sarah and Valerie had a long talk that night. Sarah wanted to work things out with Valerie once and for all. It turned out that Sarah was upset when Valerie hadn't signed up for ceramics with her, and Valerie had honestly forgotten that she had said she'd spend the last free choice period with Sarah. Sarah had started hanging out with Brynn just to get her back, and Brynn was trying to get back at Alex. It had turned into a complicated, nasty, nonfriendly mess for everyone.

"When we're mad at each other in the future, let's promise to talk it out instead of all of this dissing,"

Valerie said, attaching another carved wooden elephant to her bunk.

"Let's call ourselves the Twinkies," Alex joked.

The other girls shifted uncomfortably. Since they all had found out that Alex had juvenile diabetes, they learned that her body couldn't process sugar. They also figured out that Jenna's Twinkies the night before had probably set off Alex's diabetic attack. But no one blamed Jenna. They didn't blame Alex, either. Chelsea hadn't even piped in to offer her "advice" on what had happened. In fact, she'd been sitting on her bed by herself. Karen was starting to hang around with Natalie and Alyssa more, and Chelsea didn't seem one bit happy. Her lips were pursed and her eyes creased as she brushed her hair and pulled it into ponytails using a small hand mirror.

"It's just a joke," Alex said, laughing at their wide-eyed, afraid-to-laugh expressions. "It was meant to be funny!"

"I thought it was funny!" Candace said, laughing.

"I don't care what you all call us," Natalie said. She'd seen many friendship feuds in her private school in Manhattan. Though she would never have gotten in the other girls' business, she was more relieved than anyone to see the bunk work out their differences. "As long as you take care of yourself."

"Alex, that just can't happen again," Jenna said, changing into a pair of pajamas. Jenna had been trying to share her goodies with Alex all summer (and the summer before that). She had almost a nauseous gurgle in her stomach about it. She could've killed Alex—and she almost did yesterday. "It just can't happen again."

"It won't, I promise," Alex said, coming over to hug her friend.

They went to bed, all getting along. Tomorrow was the last day of Color War, and even though it wouldn't be the same without playing sports, Alex looked forward to much more friendly competitions.

▲ ▲ ▲

The second day of Color War was amazing. Chelsea and Alex kicked some tail at Scrabble, and Jenna kicked some butt of her own in basketball.

In the Scrabble competition that morning, Alex knew it was something they could do. Last year, she and Chelsea had picked off campers—like Gaby from 3A and Trevor from 3F—left and right. Obviously Alex and Chelsea weren't exactly friends, but when they had to, the two girls could work together. They had team spirit.

And Nurse Helen was right, the Blues in Alex's division needed a good coach—and the counselors were willing to let Alex take over. So that day, Alex stood on the sidelines strategizing, and her team always ran back to her for advice. She was so happy because she had still gotten her sports fix. And her Blues had done a terrific job that day. According to Alex's point calculations, she had an idea of which team had won. But sometimes there were surprises—like the deduction Dr. Steve had taken for the overzealous Reds who had woken up the camp—so Alex had to wait until the banquet later that day to see the final tally.

But first, there was a play to see!

Brynn and Grace's play! Alex thought, excited. She

couldn't wait to see her friends on stage.

"Okay, makeover time!" Natalie called. Natalie had a makeup kit the size of a tackle box. She'd gotten it from her famous dad's super-famous model girlfriend. It was so fancy—Alex figured the products had come straight from Rodeo Drive in Beverly Hills.

"Me!" Jenna yelled, surprising everyone. She was such a huge jock—and she didn't usually care about those things.

"Are you kidding?" Natalie said, laughing.

"Well, just a little bit of blush," Jenna answered, blushing naturally. "I thought it might be fun to try for a change."

"I'm doing my own," Alyssa said. She liked to wear black mascara really, really thick on special occasions. Candace, Jessie, and Sarah got in line next. Grace had gone first. She had the lead female part of Wendy—a *huge gigantic deal* because usually the leads went to the older kids. Grace had been so excited the past few days that she'd been waking up extra early. Brynn was excited, too—she was a Lost Boy—but she didn't have trouble sleeping in. Brynn had busily done her own eyes, cheeks, and even hair. She loved doing that stuff before her plays.

Both Grace and Brynn were already backstage, preparing for their debut. All day long, their mouths had been moving silently as they went over their lines. They were so worried that they would forget something or say the wrong line when it really mattered. The two drama divas had huddled together and seemed nervous at breakfast, especially Grace who hadn't done as much acting as Brynn had in the past. Brynn taught Grace her deep yoga breaths, and everyone laughed at them as they chanted, "Ooooommmm. Oooooommmm. Ooooommmm.".

Chelsea had a pink dress with tiny little flowers that was way fancier than what anyone else had brought. Natalie let a few of the girls, including Alex, borrow her extra skirts. Alex hadn't even brought a skirt to camp—she never did. She paired Natalie's jean skirt with one of her navy blue polo-style shirts, and checked herself in the mirror. While the other girls were cuted up with makeup and lip gloss, Alex went plain-faced. She loved being *au naturel*. Her only concession was to let Nat take out her ponytail and fluff her hair up with some gel. She dabbed on some moisturizer and was ready to go. She grabbed Valerie, and the two of them—the first ones ready in the bunk—were good to go.

"Sarah, hurry up!" Valerie said as Alex pulled her by the arm to wait for everyone outside by the door. She was impatient—like everyone else in the bunk—and ready to party!

Sarah was still standing in front of the wall-sized mirror in the hot, humid bathroom that really did need a good cleaning.

"I'm almost done!" Sarah yelled, seeing her friends heading off without her.

"It's okay. Take your time," Alex said, sitting down to wait for her friend. Sarah was soft-spoken, but very cool. She made these quiet, dry remarks that cracked Alex up.

Alex had forgotten how well she and Sarah had gotten along earlier in the summer—before Brynn went wacky on her. Alex didn't like to think about how hurt she'd been just a few days before. It was all over, and she was trying to forget. There was no sense in dwelling on the bad.

Just twenty more minutes, and Alex would see Brynn and Grace up there on stage.

"So, how do I look?" Julie asked, twirling around. Her shoulders sparkled because of all the glitter lotion she had on.

"You don't look like you're going to a play! You look like you belong in a music video," Alex said, rushing over to Julie with the rest of the girls.

"I think she's going on a date," Val said as Sarah looked at her, winking.

Julie's face turned bright red. Alex was standing next to her counselor—the one who'd secretly counseled Alex about her diabetes all summer long—and Alex noticed that Julie's skin was hot.

"You're awfully excited to see *Peter Pan* tonight. Don't you think?" Alex asked, teasing Julie.

Julie had been such a fantastic friend to Alex. She was always reminding Alex to get her insulin shots from Nurse Helen and making sure that none of the other girls heard her. Julie had tried to get Alex to tell her friends about her problem, but when Alex didn't want to, Julie respected Alex's decision.

Instead, Julie had Alex hang out in the kitchen a lot because the other counselors knew about her condition and accepted her for it. Julie figured that Alex needed a few friends who understood. She also wanted to make sure that Alex got enough to eat. Julie was always slipping Alex celery sticks and carrots and other snacks that Alex was allowed to have.

"I'm seeing my 'date' at the show!" Julie exclaimed, her blue eyes sparkling more than her shoulders.

"Who? Who?" Alex yelled.

"You have to tell us!" Valerie said, chiming in.

"Come on—just tell us!" Sarah begged.

"Oh, please," Chelsea added sarcastically, rolling her eyes. No one paid any attention to her.

"You'll find out soon enough," Julie said, spraying on just a tiny bit of perfume—too much, and the mosquitoes would eat her alive. Then she headed out the door.

The rest of the girls followed, going straight to the rec hall where *Peter Pan* was about to debut.

▲ ▲ ▲

The music came out of a CD player, but it was still amazing. The instrumentals were light and airy, as if Tinker Bell herself had been playing them. Grace did a fantastic job in her role of Wendy. Alex loved how Grace made Wendy a lot more punk and hip than she was in the original. Grace wore leg warmers and had a pink ponytail extension in her hair. But that was just like Grace; she had a way of livening everything up. Whenever she spoke on stage that night, the rest of Camp Lakeview—nearly four hundred kids—literally went silent to hear her.

Not to be left out of the spotlight, Brynn did a great job as Peter Pan's right-hand man, as well. She played Nibs, the Lost Boy who was the main character's smart and debonair best friend. Alex laughed when Tinker Bell, played by a tiny eight-year-old girl, sometimes acted like she had a crush on Nibs. Brynn's Nibs never noticed anything but his best friend—Peter Pan—and followed Peter's every order. Alex figured all those yoga breaths that Brynn did were helpful—she didn't miss one line. She even delivered her words in a brisk, deep boyish tone. Alex was astonished at how Brynn could transform herself on stage. She was so girlie in real life but such a boy when she needed to play one.

Grace's real-life crush Devon played the minor part of another Lost Boy. Sparks flew when Grace was on the stage with him (though Grace did a good job of acting like she had a thing for the boy who played Peter Pan, too). But Grace and Devon were so flirtatious and sweet that Valerie kept nudging Alex. They'd had a thing for each other for a while—that much was clear just by the way they interacted on stage.

What does it feel like to have a crush? Alex asked herself. *I don't think I get it.*

"Oh my God, did you see those two?" Val whispered in a hushed, high voice of pure disbelief. "They are so into each other!"

Alex couldn't help herself: She thought of Adam and wondered if she would ever have a crush. She just knew he liked Valerie, and she had to admit she was a little disappointed by that, which made no sense, not even to her.

Just then, the kid playing Michael, Wendy Darling's youngest, most rambunctious brother, knocked down a ten-foot cardboard ship. It was an accident, but a big one. Once the ship came down, the other set pieces—a tree, a fake crocodile, a few hooks lying around—also came down.

Alex gasped. Her heart started to sink. All of the hard work that Grace and Brynn and the rest of the cast had done was brought down into shambles.

For a moment, everyone on stage froze. It was as though no one knew what to do.

Then Grace stepped forward.

"It is now time for our intermission," she said, pulling the curtain closed. She shoved another kid, a seven-year-old girl who played Nana the dog, in front of the closed curtain. The kid stared, wide-eyed, looking as if she were about to cry. But just when everyone was least expecting it, Grace peeked her head out of the curtain and whispered something to the pint-sized dog. Then the dog started singing the song, "You Are My Sunshine." The audience—especially Alex, Valerie, and Sarah—laughed so hard that their heads almost exploded.

"Grace is awesome," Alex said, her face getting sore from so much giggling.

A few minutes later, the show went on, as the ship and other set pieces had been set back up (though they weren't as straight as they had been before). Even with a minor catastrophe, Camp Lakeview's *Peter Pan* had turned out great. It was definitely the best thing Alex had seen there.

She was so impressed with the actors—they had put so much emotion into their lines. And the set was cool, too; Sarah and Brynn had a done a fantastic job painting everything and setting it up. Alex couldn't help but think that Brynn would be a great set designer one day if she ever wanted to go that route. Brynn would be great at anything she set her mind to.

When Grace came out to take a bow after the show was over, the audience roared. Brynn bowed right after her, and Alex stood up and started a standing ovation.

Since Alex was the first out of her seat, she could see clear to the back of the room. She nudged Valerie and couldn't help but point.

"Do you see that?" Alex said, jumping up and down, for the show and for what she was witnessing.

"Oh my goodness!" Valerie said, turning bright red.

"They are so cute together," Alex said, tugging on Valerie and Sarah's arms.

Julie was sitting in the back of the room holding hands with their woodworking instructor, Jeremy. They two of them were nuzzling like love-struck puppies. Julie had never looked sparklier—and it wasn't from the lotion she had borrowed from the girls in 3C.

The applause continued throughout the drama shack. All the kids—four hundred of them—were standing and cheering for the young actors. Still smiling, Alex turned to watch Brynn and Grace take their final bows as Nibs and Wendy from *Peter Pan*.

Alex was so proud of them.

chapter

TEN

After the play, Alex rushed to the stage to hug Brynn and Grace. Then she rushed to the mess hall with Natalie and Alyssa because she was helping with the banquet dinner. She helped pull several pans of vegetable lasagna and several more pans of meat lasagna out of the oven.

Pasta was especially good for kids with diabetes—the sugar released more slowly into their bodies—and so were vegetables. So she picked her favorites to help everyone make with the meal: green beans cooked with bacon, salad with cheese, and honey cookies for dessert. (She could have those because honey was better for her than other kinds of sugar.)

Alex was more careful about what she ate than most kids with diabetes were. She figured out when she was first diagnosed that if she watched her food carefully—saying no to all the yummy stuff she really wanted to eat—she didn't have to get as many insulin shots during the day. She was down to one per day, and she didn't have to sneak off to see Nurse Helen anymore. Now that everyone knew, she could walk there without making excuses. She realized how much more relaxed she was with the counselors' support, and without having to hide or sneak off and make excuses. And most of all, without someone like Chelsea tormenting her every other day.

When Alex worked in the kitchen, she was happier than ever. She and Brynn were better. Valerie and Sarah had patched things up. The play had been awesome. And even she had to admit it: Color War was still fun, even from the sidelines.

She was suddenly surprised by a towel that snapped in her direction. The whip of it just barely missed her right knee. Pete was at the other end of the weapon, laughing his face off.

"I *know* you're not really going to get me with that thing," Alex said, grabbing a goofy-looking hairnet. She was required to wear it whenever she helped out. Pete and the others had them on, too.

"So I hear you whipped some tail at Scrabble this morning," he said, turning around to stir a huge bubbly pot of bright red tomato sauce that was making a mess all over his stove. Alex thought she had better taste it. Pete wasn't the best cook—someone might have to sneak in and fix that sauce so it didn't wind up tasting like Play-Doh. He was busy fixing extra spaghetti in case the campers ate up all the lasagna.

"I did pretty well!" Alex answered, grabbing a towel to snap him. If she got his attention away from the pot, she'd be able to sneak in and taste the sauce.

"More than *well*," Pete said, snapping her back as she washed her hands, preparing to dunk her finger.

What Pete said was true. Alex had taken the entire

Scrabble tournament that morning. She had beaten the older kids, the counselors, even Chelsea. And she was beaming about it.

She didn't want to brag or anything, so she tried really hard to beam inwardly. The thing with Chelsea had been pretty easy. They wound up playing against each other in their division—after they'd already won for the Blues. So they played it out to see who could be the ultimate winner.

Alex, Natalie, Candace, and Alyssa helped Pete and the other cooks in the kitchen for fifteen more minutes before dinner was finally ready. Alex chopped while Marissa scrambled in and out to finish setting the tables. Alex couldn't wait to sit with her friends and have fun at the formal banquet that night.

"Alex, do you want me to save you a seat?" Brynn yelled into the kitchen.

"Yes, please!" Alex yelled, taking off her hairnet and rushing out to hang with her friends.

"Where do you think you're going?" Pete asked, pretending that he was about to flip sauce onto her navy blue shirt.

"I gotta eat," she yelled, knowing that she was done for the night. She had helped plan and prepare, and now she just wanted to have some fun.

In honor of the banquet, the mess hall had been completely transformed. All of the banners that different campers had made for Color War were plastered across the wall, and red and blue streamers hung from the rafters. A centerpiece of red and blue balloons had been placed on top of every table. The entire room was abuzz with excitement—the fun and glamour of being dressed up for a special occasion, as well as the imminent announcement of the winners of Color War had everyone hopped-up like three-year-olds on a sugar rush.

"I'm sure everyone wants to know which team won the Color War," Dr. Steve said, stepping up to the front of the room with a devilish glint in his eye. Everyone clapped and cheered in anticipation. "It should be no surprise to anyone that the victors were. . . the Blues!"

The campers went crazy, stamping their feet and pounding on their tables. Dr. Steve laughed. "The point totals were . . ."—he paused, dragging the moment out for all it was worth—"Red, three-seventy-five. And Blue . . . four hundred!"

The room shook with noise and energy. The Blues—what sounded like six thousand of them—whooped and hollered. The Reds booed in good nature. They were pretty upset, because if they hadn't broken Color War rules by raiding the camp the first morning—and losing twenty-five points for their team—then there would have been a tie.

"Ha! In your faces, Red!" Chelsea shouted, pumping her fist in the air.

"No one lost, Chelsea," Brynn said. "Not really."

Green beans and dinner rolls were thrown through the air until the Julie and Marissa convinced everyone to stop before the mayhem got out of hand. Alex was glad there wasn't a food fight that particular night: She had her good clothes on for once in her life!

As the Most Valuable Players were announced—in their division, Jenna was named for the Blues—everyone cheered some more. Alex was glad that Jenna had won. Jenna had played a great game of basketball earlier that day and she had two more overall points than Alex did. When Jenna got her award—an MVP necklace made out of clay—Alex clapped the hardest.

"And we can't forget Alex Kim," Julie announced, still all rosy-cheeked. She stood up at the front of 3C's table. "She is our top-winning Scrabble player *ever*." With that announcement, Alex turned the color of a lobster and picked up a ceramic necklace Julie had made just for the occasion. The gift was so thoughtful that Alex almost cried. Even if she hadn't been able to be in ceramics for her last free choice, she still got the necklace she had wanted to make.

The winners—the Blue team—got up to serve the chocolate chip cookies to all of the losers. Alex only ate one—others had three, four, or five—and no one gave Alex any trouble about it. Not even Chelsea, who had seemingly made up with Karen. They were sitting together at the end of the table, laughing and talking. Karen was doing *a lot* of talking!

Chelsea didn't seem to mind too much. She turned to Alex. "I'm glad you're feeling better, even if I do think you cheat at Scrabble."

Alex smiled despite herself. Chelsea could always be counted on to be . . . well, Chelsea. It was almost endearing.

The mood was happy but quiet as the girls, totally exhausted but running on adrenaline, made their way back to the bunk for the last night at camp. Alex was satisfied that she had learned a lot that summer—about bullies and sports and Twinkies and friendships.

Did I learn anything about crushes? she wondered as she saw Adam walking with Jenna, whispering to her about something. They saw her looking at them, and they started coming her way. Her heart sped up by about a hundred beats.

"So, um, Adam," Alex said, her voice quivering from way too many nerves, "I heard you won blob tag for the Blues. Congrats!"

"Thanks. Can I talk to you?" he asked, his eyes serious and wide.

"Um, I guess. What do you want?"

"Uh, excuse me," Jenna said, a tad overly loud. "I have to talk to . . . Natalie!" She turned her whole body away to "subtly" give Alex and Adam some privacy.

But why? Alex wondered.

"I just, um, wanted to see if you'd be here next summer?" Adam asked her, while he bent down to tie his shoelaces. Alex could see that his hands were trembling. *Why are his hands trembling?*

"I'm here every summer. They're good about catering to kids with diabetes here, kids like me," she answered, proud to be talking about her condition in the open. She wished she had just blurted the truth out before—her summer could've been a lot easier. "I can't wait to come back here."

"Me neither," he said, looking at her.

"Cool, see you later!" Alex said, smiling as she took off toward her friends in 3C. *Next summer will be even better!* she thought.

chapter
ELEVEN

"You what?" Natalie was screaming when Alex got back into the bunk.

"I broke up with Trevor," Alyssa said. "It's the end of the summer. Why not?"

"You're such a heartbreaker!" Natalie teased Alyssa, throwing her pillow at her best-camp-friend.

"It's about time it's that way around," Alyssa answered, flipping her Day-Glo hair up into a high, messy ponytail. "I was so bummed when Adam told me said he just wanted to be friends."

Alyssa looked directly at Alex, meeting her eyes. Alex froze, but luckily, Alyssa just smiled and looked away.

Adam dumped Alyssa? Why? Alex asked herself. This certainly put a new and confusing spin on things. Alex figured she wouldn't think about it anymore. This stuff just wasn't her business.

Before Alyssa could get another word in, Natalie dove into her bed headfirst. "I can't believe the summer is over!" she whined.

"*Oh, Simon, how I love thee!*" Grace teased. "*I can't go back to Manhattan without you! My dahhhlling!*"

"*My dahhhhhhling!*" Candace yelled, getting a laugh from the rest of the bunk.

Another pillow flew into Alyssa's face, knocking her off balance and into her sheets.

"Oh, stop it," Alyssa said to everyone. "Natalie will see Simon in the fall."

"Really?" Grace asked, still beaming from her performance as Wendy. She looked happier than she had all summer.

Grace had something else to be proud of, too: She'd caught up on all of the summer homework her parents had given her. She'd be heading back to school well-prepared in the fall. Her bunkmates had enjoyed helping her when she couldn't get through a book like *Call of the Wild*. Alex had really liked getting to know Grace better. Alex was going to miss her!

"I hope we get to hang out," Natalie said. "He lives in Westport, Connecticut. That's close to New York City. We think we'll hang out in September."

Her facial expression got all dreamy. Alex was pretty sure she wasn't ready to get *that* into a boy.

"Brynn, will you be auditioning for all the school plays?" Natalie asked, clearly trying to get the attention off her romantic possibilities.

"Um, yeah, and Grace is going to audition for parts at her school, too," Brynn added while doing a post-drama-production sun salutation, a yoga move.

Brynn told Alex that it helped her calm down. Alex was used to Brynn's moves.

In the other corner of the room, Valerie was talking to Chelsea, and Karen was standing there, too. Alex definitely wanted to get the full story later.

When the excitement died down, and that took at least twenty minutes after all those honey cookies everyone had eaten, Valerie ran over to Alex and hugged her. She added, "You didn't forget, did you?"

"Of course not!" Alex reached around under her bed and dug into the large suitcase to find a few sacks she had hidden there. Inside the sacks were two wooden boxes. "Now is the perfect time."

Valerie grabbed Brynn and Sarah. The three of them came over to Alex and walked just outside the bunk.

"Don't go too far, girls," Julie yelled.

"We have to give out the bunk awards next! Alex, I think you might be getting one . . ." Marissa teased from the bathroom mirror where she was fixing her hair.

"Okay," Alex said, trembling. "This is for you." She handed one sack to Brynn.

"And this is for you," Valerie said, handing the other one to Sarah.

Both girls looked puzzled. The girls tore into them. Once they realized what the gifts were, they shrieked with excitement. "This is amazing!" Brynn said as she opened and closed the box. Hers had flowers carved on it. The wood was cedar, and Brynn stuck her nose in to take a whiff and went, "Ahhh."

"It is. But why did you do this?" Sarah said, admiring the stars and moons that were carved on her wooden box.

"There's one more, actually," Alex said, feeling suddenly shy. She dashed back into the bunk, pulled another bag out, and rushed back outside to hand it to a very surprised Valerie.

"One for me, too?" Valerie asked, bewildered. Her

box had a simple, round elephant carved on it.

"Valerie, you are awesome. Yours is a huge thank-you," Alex said, hugging her friend. She looked at the other girls.

"Brynn and Sarah, Valerie and I made these thinking that they would help us all make up and be nice to one another again—it was a gift we wanted to give you." Alex blushed, feeling like she was in an after-school television special. "Valerie thought of doing it. She's the generous one, not me," Alex said, admiring Valerie's cornrows that were piled festively on top of her head. "She's also the talented one, I mean, she taught me *how*."

Brynn wiped tears from her eyes—she really could cry on cue—and ran over to hug Alex. "This means so much to me. I'm so sorry for everything the past few weeks."

"Stop it. That's so yesterday!" Alex yelled. "I'm just glad you like it!"

Brynn reached over and hugged Valerie, too. But she had to wait her turn. Sarah was saying something to Valerie that got Valerie all teary-eyed.

"Enough of this sappy stuff," Alex said, wanting to party and not get sad. She would miss her camp friends *sooo* much.

"Wait, Alex," Brynn answered. "You're the only one without one of these!"

"No, she's not," Valerie said, smiling from cornrow to cornrow. "Here you go, girl." Valerie handed Alex a wooden jewelry box with soccer balls carved on it.

"You are too much!" Alex said, hugging Valerie.

She did feel like these girls knew her well. She didn't have anything to hide. She was sure that this summer she had belonged at Camp Lakeview. She really wanted to cry because she was so happy. But she held back—she wanted to celebrate, not get sappy.

⛺ ⛺ ⛺

After the gift exchange, Alex, Valerie, Brynn, and Sarah went back inside the bunk with the rest of 3C.

"Snack time!" Jenna yelled, pulling out a small cardboard box—the last of her snack stash.

Alex's throat tightened because that was her conditioned response. Every time Jenna had snacks, Alex would have to dodge them.

But then her muscles relaxed all over. This time was different because everyone finally knew the whole truth.

"Alex, you first," Jenna said.

Alex's throat tightened again—this time because she was surprised. Jenna knew she couldn't have any.

Alex's face scrunched up. She had hoped that awkward moments like this one were in the past. She thought it was all over!

"Just look in the box! Go on," Jenna chided, smiling and giggling. The other girls stood back like they were all in on a joke.

Alex looked in and she saw packs of sugar-free pudding. Her face broke out into an enormous grin. She reached in and took one, along with a spoon. The other girls waited their turn.

"We want you to know we love you," Brynn said, passing out the sugar-free treats to everyone.

Even Chelsea took one, looked up, and smiled at Alex. "We're with you this time."

Alex just beamed, and finally, she couldn't hold back the waterworks that gushed out of her eyes. She wiped her cheeks with the insides of her arms and then she tore open the pudding. It was the very best thing she could've eaten. And that's because she was eating it with her very best friends.

She held up her plastic tub filled with smooth chocolate yumminess and yelled, "Cheers to 3C!"

Turn the page for a sneak preview of

camp CONFIDENTIAL

TTYL

available soon!

Natalie: Saturday

Aries8: Natalie! U there?

NatalieNYC: JENNA!!! OMG, what's up? camp only ended saturday but I miss u so much already. how's home?

Aries8: ok. I'm at my dad's—totally boring. Just looking at stuff online with adam.

NatalieNYC: Hi, adam.

Aries8: He's getting food right now—I had to im u and say he got a text message from Simon last night—just saying hi and whatever and then he was like, "I am totally glad to be home—just miss my friends and obviously Natalie."

NatalieNYC: Aww, that's so sweet, J.

Aries8: Totally. R u gonna keep seeing him?

NatalieNYC: ?? Don't know. CT isn't that far but… there's Kyle. He's here, in NY, and I'm kind of into him.

Aries8: U mentioned him at camp.

NatalieNYC: Gotta go—Hannah's here, we're going back-to-school shopping!!! Totally the best thing about fall…right? talk to u on the msg board! Bye!

Aries8: I'd luv to go shopping, if I wasn't stuck at my dad's.

NatalieNYC: NATALIENYC is unavailable

Natalie couldn't believe how excited she was to see Hannah. It had only been a couple of months since Hannah had jetted off to Europe and Natalie had boarded the bus to Camp Lakeview, but it felt like a lifetime—and so much had happened in Nat's life that she knew a huge catching-up session was in order. So the obvious thing to do the second she got home from camp? Call Hannah, and invite her to go shopping the next day! Natalie was beyond thrilled to be back in New York City, where no one considered denim overalls and a tank top to be the height of fashion.

She'd brought tons of cute summer outfits to camp, but she never wore any of them, except to the camp-wide social events. And school was going to start on Tuesday—the day after Labor Day, she'd officially be in middle school—so she definitely needed new fall clothes.

Plus, the day before, when they'd talked on the phone, Hannah had told her about a school social being held for all incoming sixth-graders on the first Friday back—just one more reason to get a new, cute outfit.

Natalie was online, talking to Jenna, when she heard the door buzzer ring at the Upper West Side apartment she shared with her mom. She was practically out of the computer room before she remembered to say good-bye to Jenna. She ran down the hallway to the living room, super excited to see her best friend.

Hannah was standing in the cream-colored foyer, wearing a little purple miniskirt and a black top and talking to Natalie's mom, who was still in her pajamas even though it was after noon.

For the umpteenth time, Nat was reminded of how great it was to be back—she and her mom had brunched on bagels and veggie cream cheese, watched a couple of cartoons, and just taken it easy for the morning. It had been so long since Natalie had slept past seven that her body automatically woke her up—but she'd ignored the internal alarm, rolled over, and promptly fallen asleep.

"Hannah!" Natalie shrieked.

"Natalie!" Hannah screamed.

The two girls leaped at each other, hugging ferociously. "Oh my god, it is so good to see you, Nat!" Hannah said. "I thought this day would never come!"

Natalie laughed. "So melodramatic," she said teasingly. "Some things never change. I'm beyond thrilled to see you, too—but I gotta tell you, seeing your adorable skirt—I'm pretty anxious to get out and get shopping!"

Natalie's mom laughed. "She means she's anxious to tell you all about the boy she met this summer, Hannah. And to buy clothes."

She crossed the living room and picked up her purse from the red easy chair that was Natalie's favorite place in the house to curl up and read a magazine.

Drawing out her wallet from the bag, she looked up at Natalie. "You know the budget, Nat," she said, handing over a credit card. "And make sure you try everything on."

Nat just rolled her eyes good-naturedly. "Oh, I will, Mom . . ." she said. As she and Hannah went out the door, she leaned back in and said, "And don't worry—I'll try on everything I see!"

Her mom laughed, and Nat closed the door. She and Hannah headed to the elevator bank.

"I swear," Natalie joked, "I pretty much forgot how to use an elevator—I couldn't remember what floor we lived on for a minute!"

"Then your mom reminded you about takeout, right?" Hannah teased her. "What was the first thing you ordered?"

"Spicy tuna roll . . . mmm . . ." Natalie said, smiling and closing her eyes at the memory. "Edamame . . . miso . . . red bean ice cream . . ."

"Snap out of it, sushi girl," Hannah said. The green light above one of the elevators blinked. "You remember how to get to the lobby?"

"Ha-ha," Nat said.

In the lobby, Charles, the doorman, held the door and tipped his hat as the two girls sauntered out to the street. "Good-bye, ladies," he said. Winking at Natalie, he added, "And welcome home!"

"Thanks, Charles," Natalie replied. "Have a great day!"

On the sidewalk, she looked at Hannah. "Uptown, or down?"

"Oh, you've been out of the City longer than I have," Hannah responded, shielding her eyes with her hand and looking up and down the street at the passersby. "You choose."

"Hannah, you've only been back for a week!"

"I know, but you've only been back for, like, less than twenty-four hours."

Natalie laughed. "Good point. Okay, down. It's gorgeous out—want to walk?"

"Sure," Hannah said easily.

The girls walked in silence for a few minutes, and Natalie looked up at all the buildings. She couldn't believe how *tall* everything was, after a summer in a place where the highest things around were trees, not huge skyscrapers. All around her, there were crowds of people, pushing and walking and biking and driving. At camp, there had been lots of campers—but nothing like this. The city felt hectic, claustrophobic, even.

Natalie *loved* it.

Hannah looked over at her. "So I ran into Kyle Taylor the other day," she said, breaking the silence. "At the Boathouse in Central Park—he was there with his big brother."

"Really?" Natalie said. "I expected to hear from him at least a couple of times over the summer. I was sort of disappointed when I didn't," she admitted.

"Yeah, I know. He told me he left the address at school on the last day and couldn't get anyone to let him in to get it. He looked really miserable about it." Hannah stopped before crossing the street, and looked at Natalie playfully. "Remember how to tell if you can walk?" she teased.

"Yeah, it's the big orange hand, right?" Natalie deadpanned. She was quiet for a moment. "So . . . what else did he say about me?" The light changed, and they walked on.

"Nothing. I told him when you were coming back and that was basically it, because his brother came, and they left."

"Oh." Natalie considered this for a minute. "So . . . do you think he's still interested?"

"I don't know, Nat," Hannah said—sort of evasively, Natalie thought. "Probably."

Before Natalie could continue, Hannah pointed off to her right. "Hey," she said, stopping in front of a boutique they'd been to before. "Let's go in here."

"Okay," Natalie said. "So, what do you think—"

"Wow, back-to-school sale!" Hannah said.

Okay, Natalie thought. *Am I crazy or is she changing the subject?*

She shrugged off the weird feeling and headed toward the sale racks in the back of the store, where Hannah had already pulled a gorgeous blue sweater down and was checking the size. "Hannah, that's fantastic," Natalie said, trying to push her worries aside. "You've got to get it!" Hannah slipped the sweater over her head, and though it was the wrong color to wear with her miniskirt, the sweater looked amazing on her.

"Does it come in my size?" Natalie asked, and Hannah laughed. It was just like old times. Natalie started to relax, and started digging through the rack.

Jenna:
Saturday Night

Jenna looked over at her brother Adam, who was lying on the couch in their dad's basement, reading some new manga he had brought along for the weekend. She sighed loudly, and when he didn't look up or comment, she sighed again, louder this time.

Finally, Adam looked up. "What's wrong with you?" he asked, sounding annoyed.

"I'm so bored, Ad," Jenna replied, hoping her voice sounded as pitiful as she felt.

She could not believe that she was stuck at her dad's new place on her first Saturday night back from camp—in a town where she didn't know anyone but her two brothers and her sister, and where there was absolutely. Nothing. To. Do.

The night before hadn't been bad; it'd been two months since the four kids were together, and it was great to see their dad. They had stayed up really late—later than their mom ever would have let them—and watched talk shows and the late movie and told their dad all about camp. And then they'd slept in, which was great after getting up at the crack of dawn all summer.

But then Saturday had rolled around, and Jenna found herself wanting to die from the boredom.

"Why don't you watch TV?" Adam suggested. He rolled over onto his stomach and looked back down at his comic book.

Jenna sighed for a third time. "Adam, you know Dad doesn't have the cable hooked up yet."

"So? Watch network," Adam said. "You've been at camp. Pretend you're roughing it."

"It's Saturday night!" Jenna cried. "There's nothing on network. *Nothing*. Maybe, like, some Hallmark Hall of Fame movie. Anyway, I don't feel like watching TV. We've been staring at that screen all day."

She knew she had a point there. After breakfast, their dad had insisted on taking them to Blockbuster, where they'd rented more movies than they could ever watch in a weekend. Even a weekend in a boring town where they didn't know anyone and where there wasn't anything to do.

The five of them had watched one movie, but then Steph and Matt had escaped to the mall, and Dad had gone upstairs to do some more unpacking and decorating.

That was seven hours ago. Jenna and Adam hadn't left the basement since. At around one, their dad had brought down a piping hot pizza he'd made from scratch, plus a two-liter of soda. He'd stayed for a half hour or so talking with them, but then he'd gone back up to clean. Jenna and Adam hadn't had the heart to tell him their mom had taken them out for pizza before dropping them off the night before. But even worse than that was the interminable boredom that set in when their dad went upstairs to clean.

Just thinking about how bored she was made Jenna feel worse. "Adddaaaaam," Jenna whined. "Can't we, like, play cards or something?"

Adam looked over his comic at her. "If Dad has cards, they're not unpacked," he said. "We've ransacked this place. Come on, just check your e-mail or something."

"I already did. When did Steph and Matt say they were coming home? Maybe they'll take us out."

Adam snorted. "To where, a movie and pizza?"

Jenna flopped onto the floor. "Even driving around would be better than this," she said.

Just then, she heard a car pull up overhead. Jumping up and clapping her hands together, she said, "Thank God! They're back!" Adam didn't respond, just rolled over onto his back.

Jenna ran up the stairs, taking two at a time. "Steph! Matt!" she called excitedly. "Do you guys want to—" When she reached the living room, she stopped. The door was wide open, but looming inside the entrance was a guy who was definitely not one of her siblings. It was a pizza delivery guy. With a big cardboard pizza box in one hand, and a two-liter bottle of soda in a plastic bag in the other.

"Look, Jen!" her dad said, beaming. "I ordered us a pizza!" He handed some folded cash to the pizza guy, who handed over the food and then shoved the money in his pocket, turned, and left. Jenna's dad swung the door closed and carried the food into the kitchen. Jenna followed, and in the kitchen, sank into a chair while her dad opened cabinets, taking down plates and glasses.

"And," her dad said, looking proud, "open up the freezer! There's a surprise in there, too!"

Jenna sighed and got up. When she opened the freezer, she gasped—it was absolutely chock-full of tons of different flavors of ice cream. Her dad laughed out loud. "I figured you probably didn't get much ice cream at camp," he said. "So I thought I'd make up for it."

"Wow, Dad," Jenna said slowly. "You certainly did." She sat back down at the table. "But this smells delicious," Jenna went on quickly, recovering.

She opened a box and slid out a piece of pizza, putting it into her mouth without blowing on it. She was rewarded with a huge pizza burn on the roof of her mouth. She chewed and swallowed quickly as tears welled up in her eyes. "Seriously, it's great," she said, trying not to cry.

Her dad looked up hopefully. "I was thinking that after dinner, we could get out the Scrabble board and play," he said. "You and me, and Adam if he wants to. What do you say?"

"That sounds great," Jenna responded, thinking: *Anything's better than another movie.*

Her dad reached out and fluffed her hair. "Great, kiddo," he said. "Why don't you run and get Adam for dinner?"

On her way down to the basement, Jenna heard a car pulling into the driveway. "Are they back?" Adam called up to her, hearing her footsteps on the stairs.

"I think so," Jenna said, walking over to sit next to him. "Listen, Ad . . . Dad got pizza for dinner. That car we heard before was the delivery guy."

Adam looked at her in disbelief. "Are you kidding me?" he said, putting down his comic book. "That's, like, three meals in a row."

"Yeah, I know," Jenna said. She rolled her eyes. "He's trying to be Superdad or something. How much do you want to bet he tries to take us to the zoo tomorrow, or something?"

"Seriously," her brother said. He sat up. "On the other hand, though, Mom hardly ever gets us pizza.

Maybe this'll be nice—kind of break up the monotony of Mom's chicken and rice, chicken and noodles, chicken and potatoes . . ." Jenna laughed. "Chicken with asparagus . . ." Adam went on.

Jenna picked up a couch pillow and whacked him with it. "Come on, loser," she said. "Let's go eat. And then I'll kick your butt at Scrabble."

"I can hardly wait," Adam said drily. He got up off the couch, though, and Jenna followed him upstairs to the kitchen.

▲ ▲ ▲

After dinner, Jenna retreated to the bedroom she was sharing with Steph. She lay down on her bed feeling overstuffed and exhausted.

After a few minutes, Steph walked in. "What's up with you?" her sister asked, sounding concerned.

"Nothing," Jenna replied. "I'm just tired."

"Look, Jen, I know it's a little dull here. And don't think it's escaped me that this is the third meal of pizza we've had in the last two days. But try to be a good sport. Dad's having a rough time right now."

"Aren't you bored, too, Steph?" Jenna asked, sitting up on the bed.

"Yes. I totally am. Do you know what I did today?"

"No," Jenna admitted. She looked up at her sister. "What did you do?"

"I went to the mall with Matt, who just wanted to ditch me and go hang out at the Discovery store or something. So I went to Barnes & Noble and read magazines. Like *all* the magazines. I was starting on

Outdoor Living when Matt finally came and asked if we could go home."

"Oh," Jenna said. "I guess it was a pretty awful day for everyone."

"Yeah, it was. Now, can you come back down and play Scrabble with us?" Steph said, crossing her arms and tapping her foot impatiently. "Seriously. Dad really wants to."

Jenna got up. "Yeah, totally," she said.

The two girls walked to the living room, where Adam had set up a card table and was placing chairs around it. Their dad walked out of the kitchen with a huge bowl of popcorn. Catching Jenna's eye, he smiled. "Nobody wanted pizza for dessert," he said. "Guess we just have to eat ice cream and popcorn."

Grace:
Monday

To: **Grrrace@internet.com**
From: **BrynnWins@internet.com**
Subject: **Miss you!**
Monday, September 3

Hey, Grace,

Can you believe school is about to start already? We've only been home for a few days, barely any time to relax, and all of a sudden we have to start getting up early again! I've really loved being able to sleep in again, though . . . and watch TV and go shopping . . .

But I am excited to go back to school. It's going to be so cool this year! At my school, since it's so small, the sixth-graders aren't at middle school—they're still at the elementary school, and next year we go to the high school. So this year, we rule! I can't wait.

Are your parents going to let you join drama club? I bet they will . . . once they see you perform, they can't possibly say no! You were the best actress at camp!

My mom is calling—we have a Labor Day barbecue thing over at my grandma's house, so I'd better go. Write back soon!

Love,
Brynn

Grace sat patiently as her mom slid two strips of bacon next to the steaming-hot eggs already on the plate in front of her. Across the table, her dad was paging through the newspaper and sipping a cup of coffee. "Grace," he said, poking his head over the paper, "what's a five-letter word for *mad*, first letter *L*?"

Grace thought for a minute. "I have no idea, Dad, sorry," she said. Her dad sighed and went back to the paper.

"Livid," her mom said, sitting down next to Grace with a plate of food for herself. "Need juice, Gracie?"

"I'll get it," Grace said. She got up and crossed to the refrigerator.

"So, Grace," her father said, folding up his newspaper and looking at her with a serious expression, "ready for the first day of school?"

Grace found the carton of orange juice behind a stack of Tupperware and sat back down at the table. "Definitely!" she said. "I finished my last book last night. *Bridge to Terabithia*. I loved it."

"That's wonderful, honey," her mom said. "I'm very proud of how hard you've worked this summer. You'll be perfectly ready to get back to school."

"Definitely," Grace said again. "I am so excited. In middle school they have drama club, and I'm signing up first thing tomorrow! I can't wait! Plus, I haven't seen any of my friends, and it's going to be so cool to . . ."

She stopped when she noticed her parents exchanging one of their famous looks. "What, you guys?" she asked, suddenly worried. "I don't like the look of those looks," she joked, trying in vain to lighten the mood.

Her mom sighed. "It's just . . . drama club? Grace, I don't think it's a good idea for you to join the drama club this year."

Grace put down her glass. "What? Why not?" she asked.

"Your mother and I think you need to focus on getting your grades up," her dad responded. "You did a great job this summer with your reading, but you have to prove that you can continue working hard. We would hate for you to take on too much too soon—and have your schoolwork suffer."

"But Dad, it won't suffer! I *will* keep working hard, I swear!" Grace promised. She could feel her face starting to turn red—a sure sign she was about to cry. "You saw how well I did this summer—I can keep working hard *and* join the drama club."

Grace's father shook his head. "Grace, I'm sorry. I'm not going to back down on this one. Camp is not the same as school—*middle school*," he reminded her. "It's not forever, sweetie, but it is for now."

Grace looked at her mom. "Mom? Please?"

"No, honey, I'm sorry. Your dad and I discussed this already; we decided that you wouldn't be allowed to join any extracurricular activities until we see real evidence that your grades are going up. That means at least one semester. I'm very sorry, and I am very proud of how well you've done so far."

Grace could tell that her mom *was* sorry, but she still couldn't believe they weren't going to let her join the club. Over the summer, she had realized how much she loved to act—she loved being onstage, with people watching her while she performed. It was an amazing rush. A tear slipped down her cheek, and she shoved her plate away and stood up so fast that her chair fell over.

"I can't believe this!" she exclaimed. Her chin began to tremble, and she had to rush away before she completely broke down into tears.

▲ ▲ ▲

Once upstairs, Grace threw herself onto her bed, buried her face into her pillow, and sobbed. *This stinks*, she thought. She rolled over, still with tears streaming down her cheeks, and sat up. Doing so, she caught a glimpse of her summer reading books, stacked neatly on her desk next to her computer.

She scrambled up and crossed her room, sliding onto the chair at her desk. She logged on to instant messenger, but none of her friends were online. *Great*, she thought. *No friends, no drama club.* She opened up her Web browser and tried to distract herself. She had gotten a really nice e-mail from Brynn earlier, but she didn't feel like writing back to it—Brynn had sounded excited about school starting, and Grace was decidedly Unexcited.

Just then, she remembered the blog that Julie, the counselor she'd had at camp, had set up for all the bunkmates to keep in touch when they got back to their own lives. Grace accessed the site, and found three messages waiting. One was a welcome note from Julie, which included Julie's e-mail address, phone number, and mailing address. There was another message from Marissa, the CIT from their bunk, but Grace was the most excited about the message from her friend Alex:

Dear 3C:

I hope everybody's having a great time back at home! I know you all miss getting up at the crack of dawn, smelling funny, and eating terrible, disgusting, horrible food. I do, too. Anyway, I just wanted to write to tell you all that I miss you so much . . . and I hope we can get together soon! Let's keep in touch here as much as possible—I want to hear about everyone's sixth-grade experience!

Love,
Alex

Grace sighed. She was sure other people *were* glad to be back with their friends—and she was, too—but she really wasn't looking forward to the sixth-grade experience. Even if she was starting to like reading more, school just wouldn't be fun without drama class. She logged off the computer without writing a response to Alex.

On the desk, next to her stack of books, was a picture from camp that Grace had framed when she got home. It was the cast from the camp play. She picked up the frame and looked closely at the picture. *I look so happy,* she thought. *And part of it was that I thought I'd be able to be in drama club this year.* She sighed and put down the photograph.

Then a thought crossed her mind. She knew both of her parents wouldn't be home from work until five-thirty each night, and this year, they'd decided she was too old for a babysitter. They'd given her a key and everything.

And drama club was after school every afternoon from three to five o'clock.

So . . . her mind was whirling. With no parents or babysitter home after school, no one would know what time she came home. And if she came home right away after drama, they would just assume she'd been there since three o'clock! *It's the perfect plan!* she thought excitedly. A tiny twinge of guilt stabbed at her sides, but she quickly waved it off. She'd keep up with her schoolwork, of course, for the semester. Then when she got all A's—or mostly A's, anyway—even *with* drama club, her parents would know that she could handle both. How could they argue?

It could work. Her plan could definitely work.

It was just a matter of pulling it off.

Alex: Tuesday

BEEP
BEEP
BEEP

Alex groaned and rolled over to swat her alarm clock. "Six-thirty already?" she moaned. It was the first day of school and she was already ready for summer vacation to swing around again.

Pulling herself out of bed, she stumbled out the door and down the hall to the bathroom. After a nice hot shower, she knew she'd start to feel like herself again.

After her shower, she pulled on the outfit she'd decided on the night before: Her favorite jeans and a cool yellow shirt she'd gotten at the mall with her mom over the weekend. She blow-dried and brushed her long brown hair and pulled it back into a ponytail, and for the finishing touch, added a pair of white socks with little frogs on them and her favorite green sneakers. Appraising herself in the full-length mirror that hung in the hallway, she thought to herself, *Perfect!* She was ready to face middle school.

Downstairs, her mother had poured a bowl of cereal for her and set it on the table with a glass of orange juice. "Eat up, Alex," her mom said. "Excited about school?"

"Yeah!" Alex replied, sitting down and taking a big gulp of juice. "Totally. I got an e-mail yesterday about soccer tryouts, too—they're today after school. So I won't be home till five."

Alex's mother put down the newspaper she was reading. "That's very exciting, honey," she said. "Do you know anyone else who's trying out?"

"Well, I think a lot of the girls from last year's team will try out," Alex said. Just then, Alex's father walked into the kitchen jangling his keys.

"Ready to go, Al?" he said. He leaned over and kissed Alex's mom and then looked at Alex expectantly. "We'd better get a move on if you're going to be at school on time."

Alex shoveled a few more spoonfuls of cereal into her mouth and then stood up to kiss her mom good-bye. She grabbed her brand-new backpack off the floor where she'd placed it the previous day and shifted it onto her shoulders. "Ready!"

The drive to school didn't take long. Alex's dad gave her a few dollars for lunch and she excitedly ran into the school lobby. Instantly, though, as she entered the crowded room, she knew she was more worried than she had let on. There were so many people packed in—and they were all so *old!* She felt like a baby. All the other kids were taller and bigger than she was. The boys looked like grown men, and the girls looked like adult women. Some of the boys even had *mustaches!* And the girls . . . well, they were obviously not in elementary school anymore.

In the corners of the room, Alex could see small groups of what had to be sixth-graders, all huddled together, looking young and scared. She stood stock-still and scanned the room, looking for a familiar face. Finally, she saw one across the room—her best friend, Ellen. Ellen's eyes met Alex's, and obvious relief flooded both their faces. *Thank goodness,* Alex thought. She was glad they had planned their meeting place the night before on the phone. She scurried over to her friend.

"Hi!" Ellen squealed, throwing her arms around Alex for a big hug. "Can you believe this place? I'm going to need some kind of personal OnStar system just to find my way around!"

Alex opened her mouth to agree, but she was cut off by a burst of static, followed by a thundering voice that boomed over the loudspeaker. "ALL STUDENTS TO THE GYMNASIUM," the deep voice said. "ALL STUDENTS TO THE GYMNASIUM FOR WELCOME ASSEMBLY." Ellen and Alex looked at each other.

"That's us," Alex said nervously.

Ellen laughed. "Oh, come on, Alex. It'll be fun!" She looped her arm through her friend's and propelled them both toward the gym, where the other students were beginning to gather. They made their way through the packed room and found seats on the end of the bleachers farthest from the door.

Looking around the room, Alex was surprised that the school's cheerleaders and sports teams had already started to work on school spirit—the walls were plastered with GO ROCKETS! LAUNCH! THREE TWO ONE BLASTOFF! and other signs supporting the football, volleyball, and, Alex realized, soccer teams. She was about to point that out to Ellen when the principal, Mr. Delaney, walked to a podium in the middle of the gym floor and began to speak.

"Welcome back, kids," his voice droned. "We hope you had a fun, safe, and educational summer." He winked as if to show that he knew the *educational* part was a stretch.

At this, some of the older boys laughed, and a boy behind Alex said to his friend, "Well . . . fun, anyway!"

"A few reminders: First tryouts for the girls' soccer team are tonight, on the main field, at three P.M. Those who make it past cuts will meet tomorrow after school. . . ."

He went on talking, but Alex had stopped listening. First *tryouts?* she thought frantically. *Since when is there more than one round?*

Suddenly, she was very, very nervous. She tuned back in to the assembly just in time to hear Mr. Delaney finish talking. "Please go to homeroom, where you will receive your schedules and locker assignments."

Luckily, Alex knew where her homeroom was— during the previous year, her class had come to the middle school to take a tour and learn their way around. She and Ellen stood up and headed in the direction of the science wing, where their rooms were. Because Ellen's last name was in the end of the alphabet, she'd been placed into a different room—but Alex figured she'd still have some classes with her friend. She also had expected to know at least a few kids in her homeroom, but she didn't. Everyone was either older or from a different elementary school. She sat down near the front of the classroom and smiled tentatively at the girl sitting next to her, but the girl just looked at her and then looked away.

Alex sighed and looked away again. Soccer tryouts—*first* tryouts, she corrected herself—weren't until the end of the day. And it was going to be a very long day, indeed.